THIS WAY TO
HAPPYVILLE

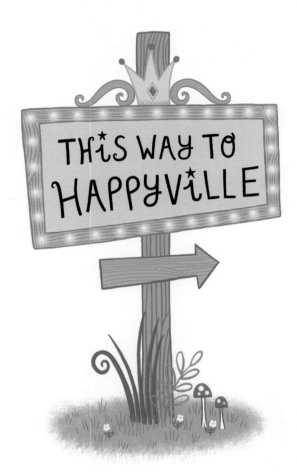

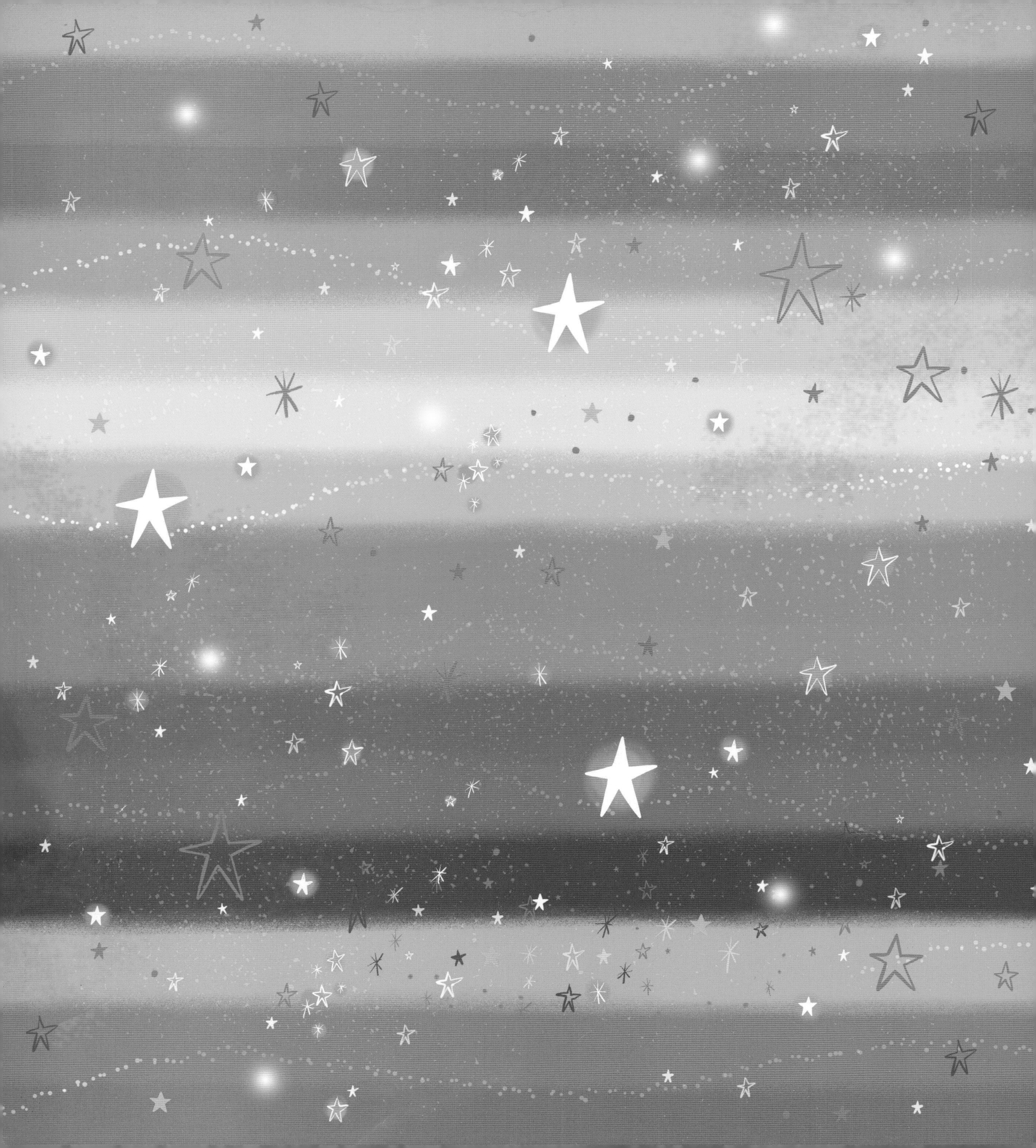

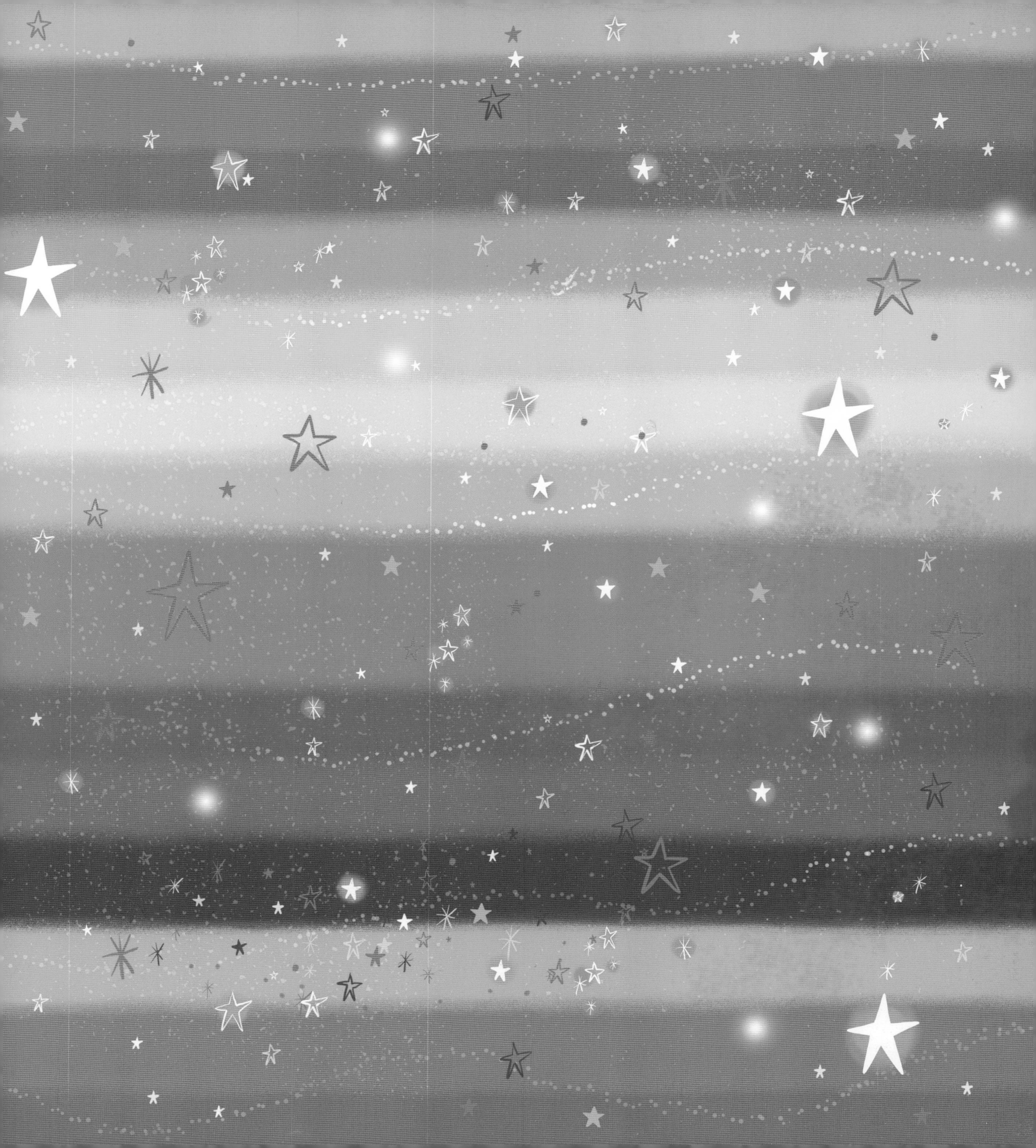

For Taylor, Lewis, Tegan and Brody,
Ellesse and Ebi-Rose, Ethan and Eryn.
With all my love, Nanny McFiz – EA

For Theia-Louise, may all your dreams sparkle – KH

First published in 2018 by Scholastic Children's Books
Euston House, 24 Eversholt Street
London NW1 1DB
a division of Scholastic Ltd
www.scholastic.co.uk
London – New York – Toronto – Sydney – Auckland
Mexico City – New Delhi – Hong Kong

Text copyright © Emma Adams
Illustrations copyright © Katy Halford

Trade Edition ISBN: 9780702300103
Scholastic Clubs and Fairs Edition ISBN: 9781407199221

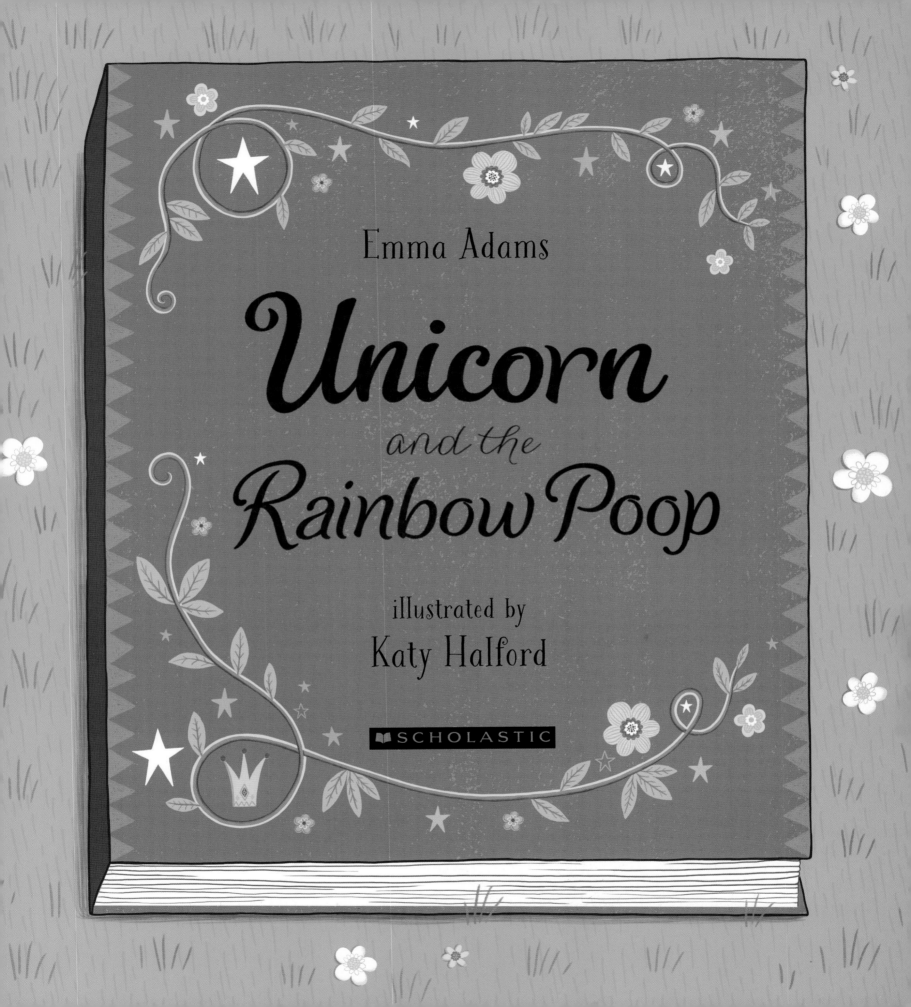

Emma Adams

Unicorn
and the
Rainbow Poop

illustrated by
Katy Halford

SCHOLASTIC

In a magical place, in a land far away,
was a small, peaceful town at the edge of a bay.
The sun shone out brightly, the sky was so blue.
And whoever lived there? Well, let me tell you . . .

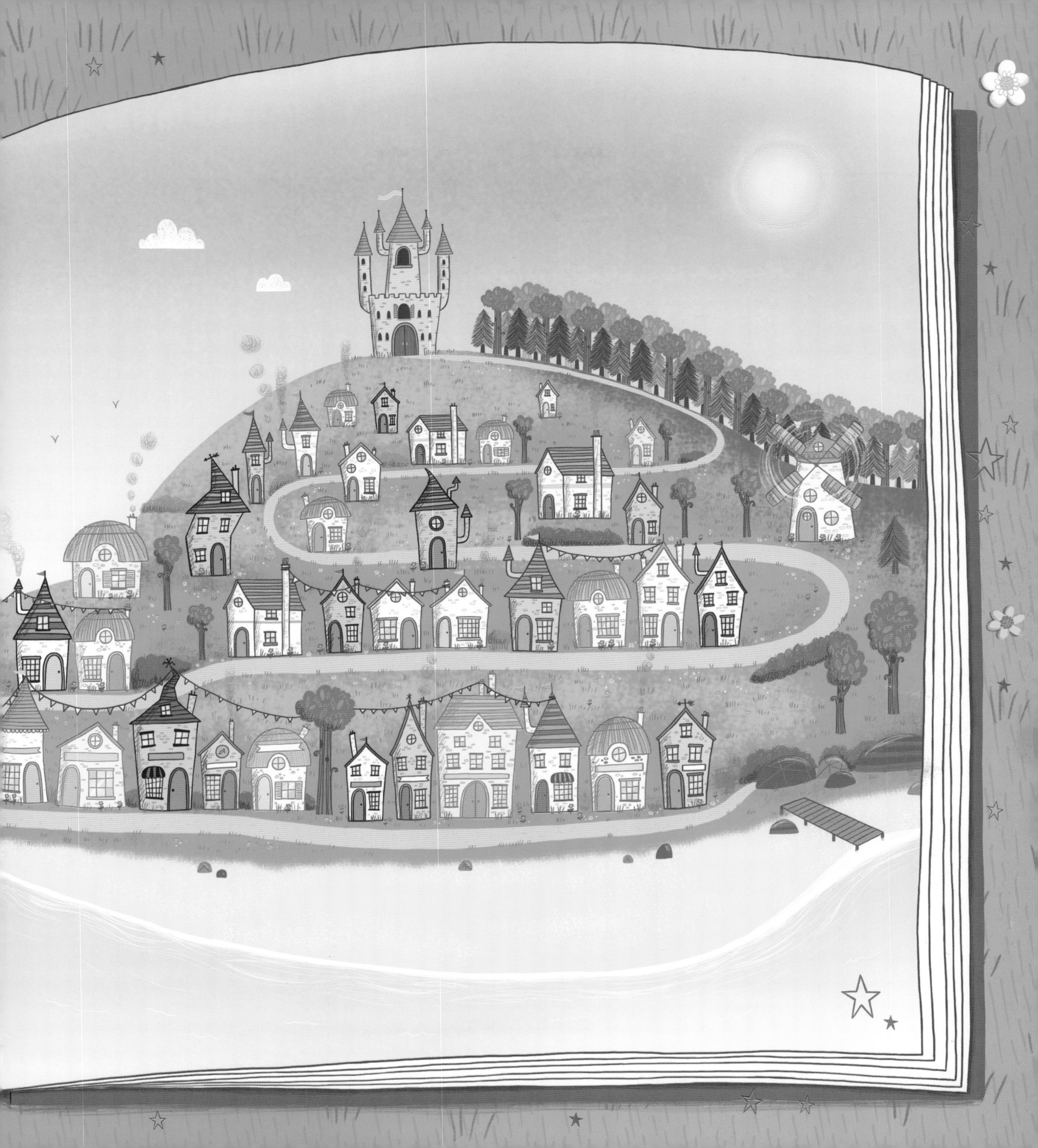

There were . . .

Princesses (many),
big **dragons** (a few)

and **witches** (the good kind,
but some bad ones too).

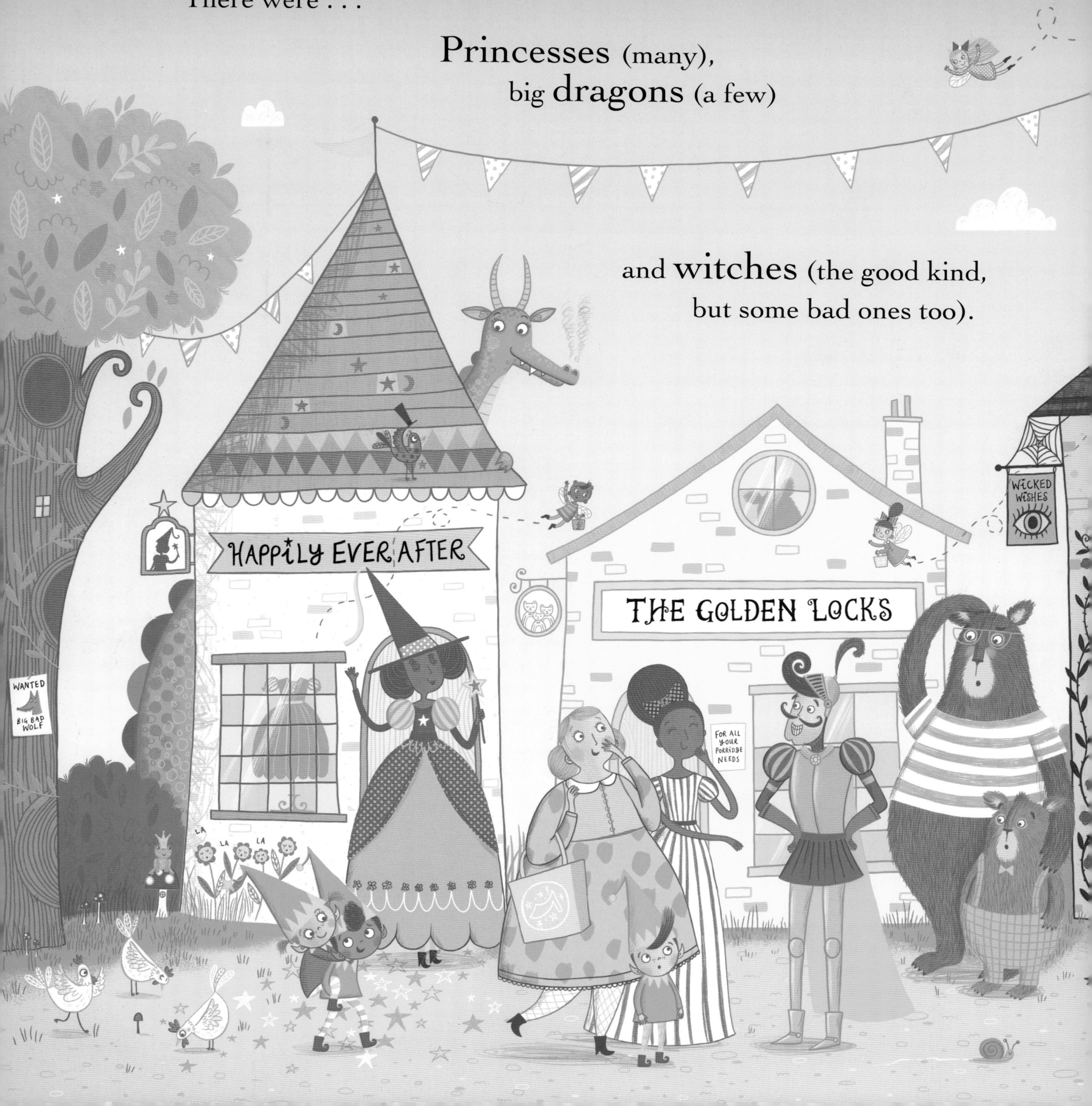
HAPPILY EVER AFTER
THE GOLDEN LOCKS
WICKED WISHES
WANTED
BIG BAD WOLF
FOR ALL YOUR PORRIDGE NEEDS
LA
LA
LA

Fairies with wings,
and birds fiery red.

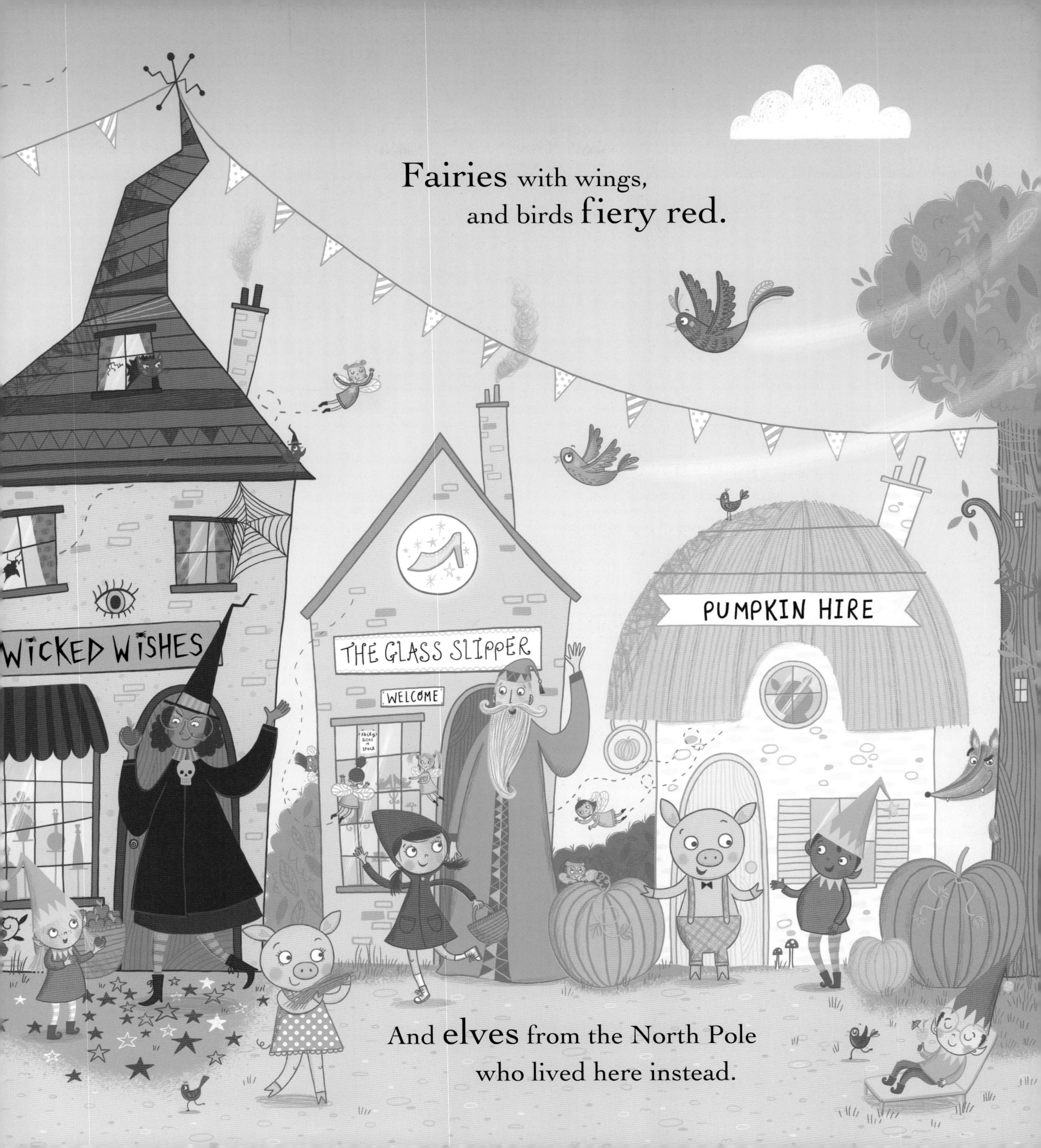
WICKED WISHES
THE GLASS SLIPPER
WELCOME
PUMPKIN HIRE

And elves from the North Pole
who lived here instead.

One morning when Princess was shining her crown, she heard someone say,

"There's a new girl in town!"

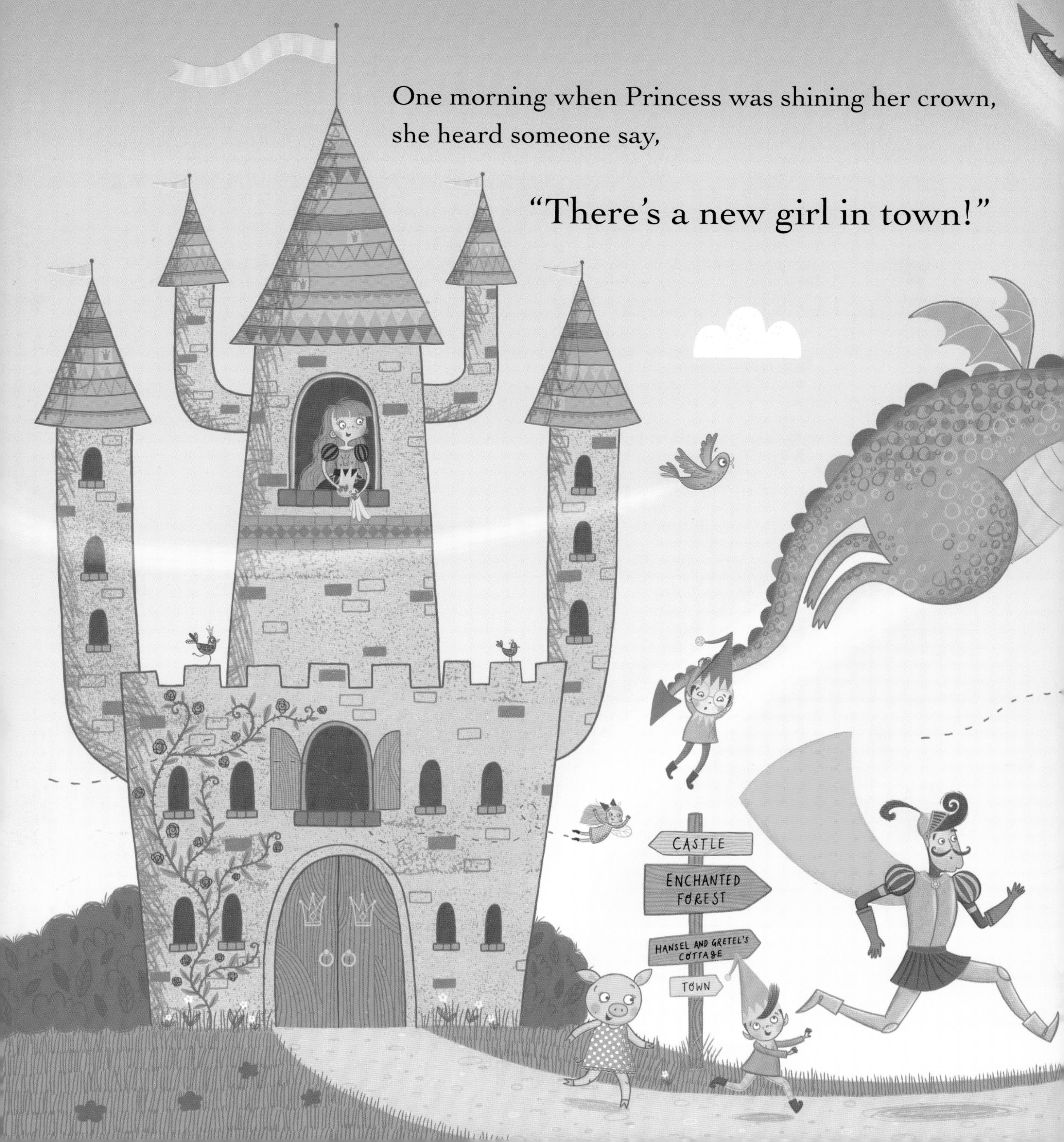
CASTLE
ENCHANTED FOREST
HANSEL AND GRETEL'S COTTAGE
TOWN

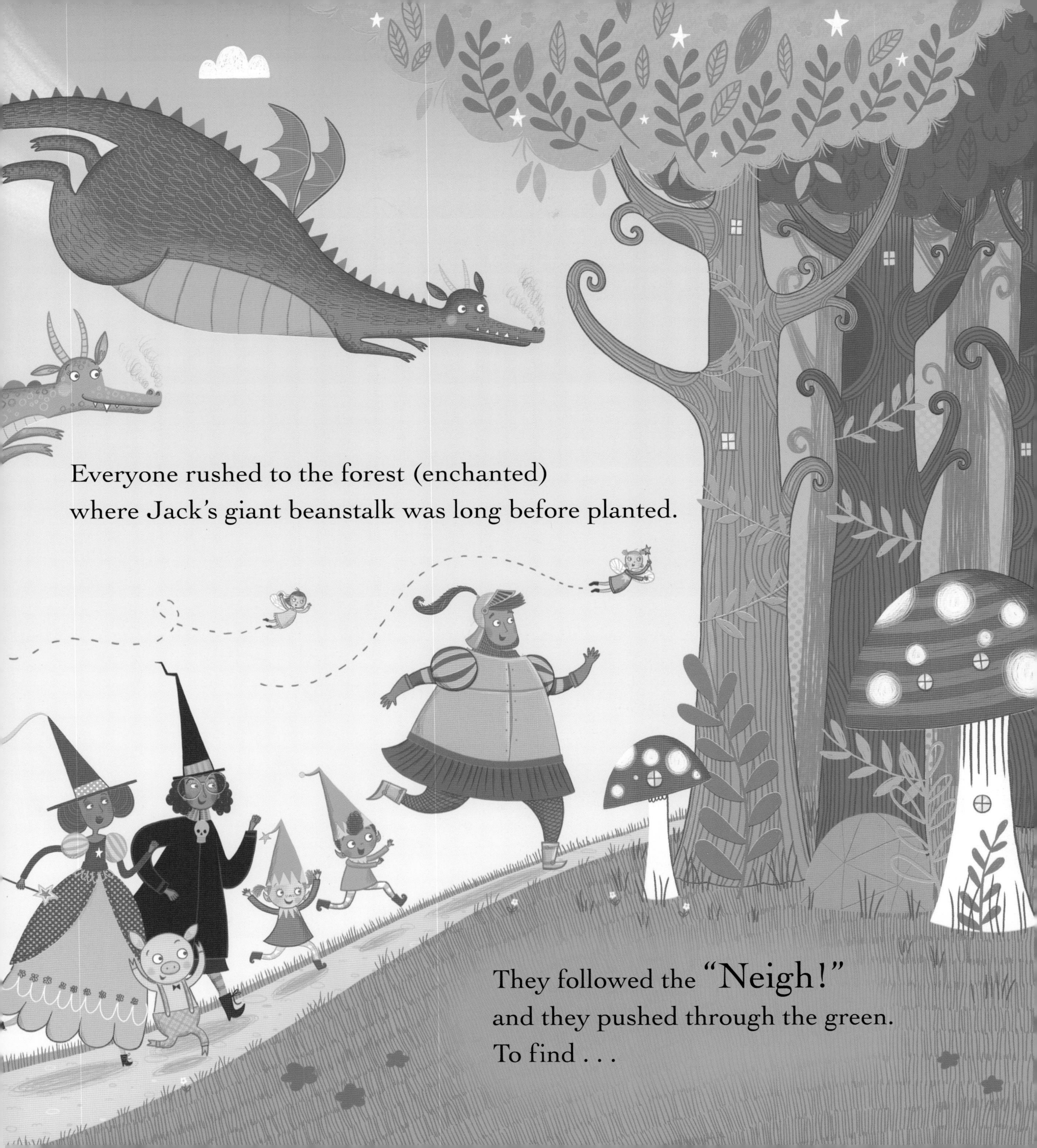

Everyone rushed to the forest (enchanted)
where Jack's giant beanstalk was long before planted.

They followed the "Neigh!"
and they pushed through the green.
To find . . .

. . . The best **unicorn**
they'd ever seen!

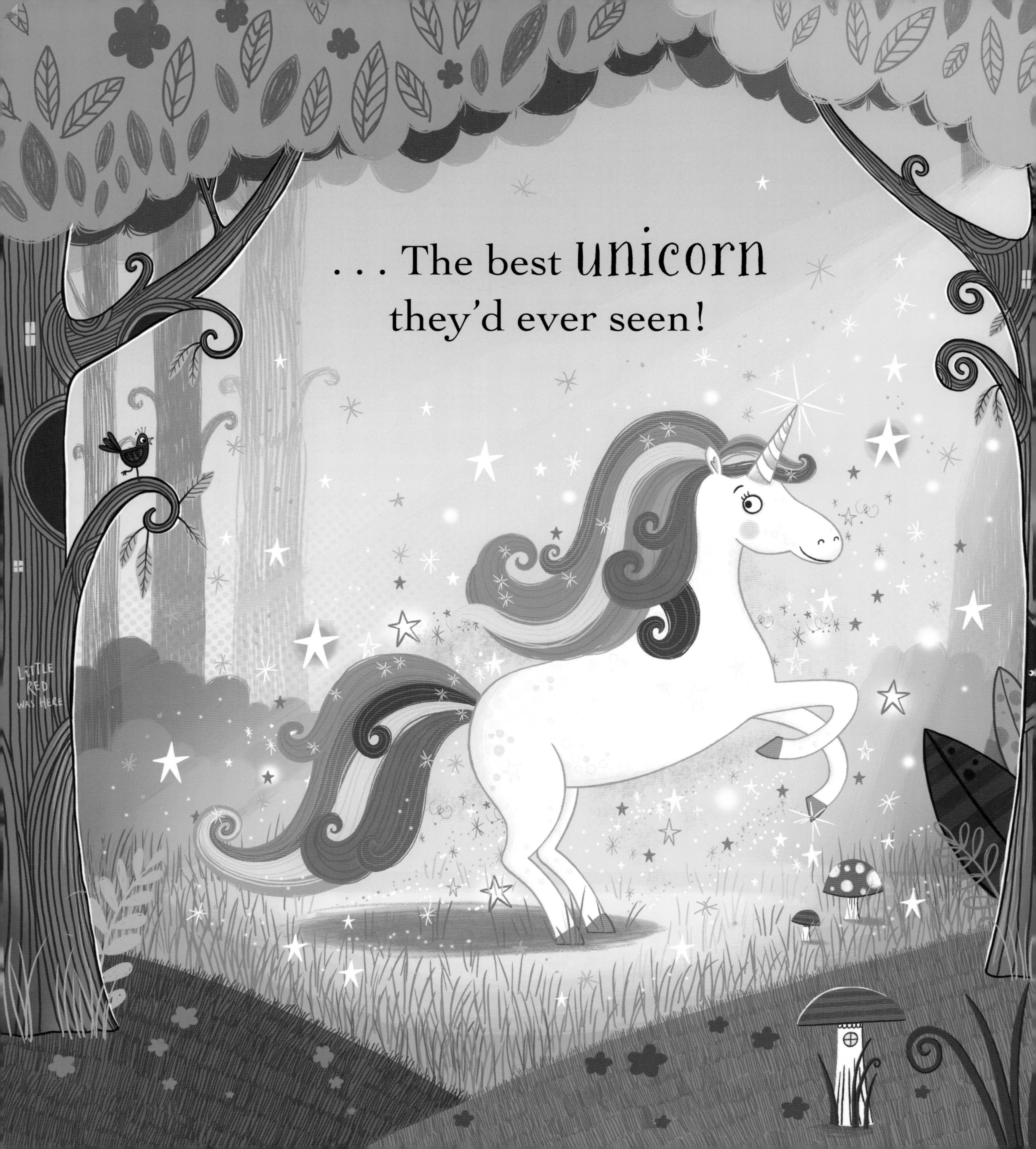
LITTLE RED WAS HERE

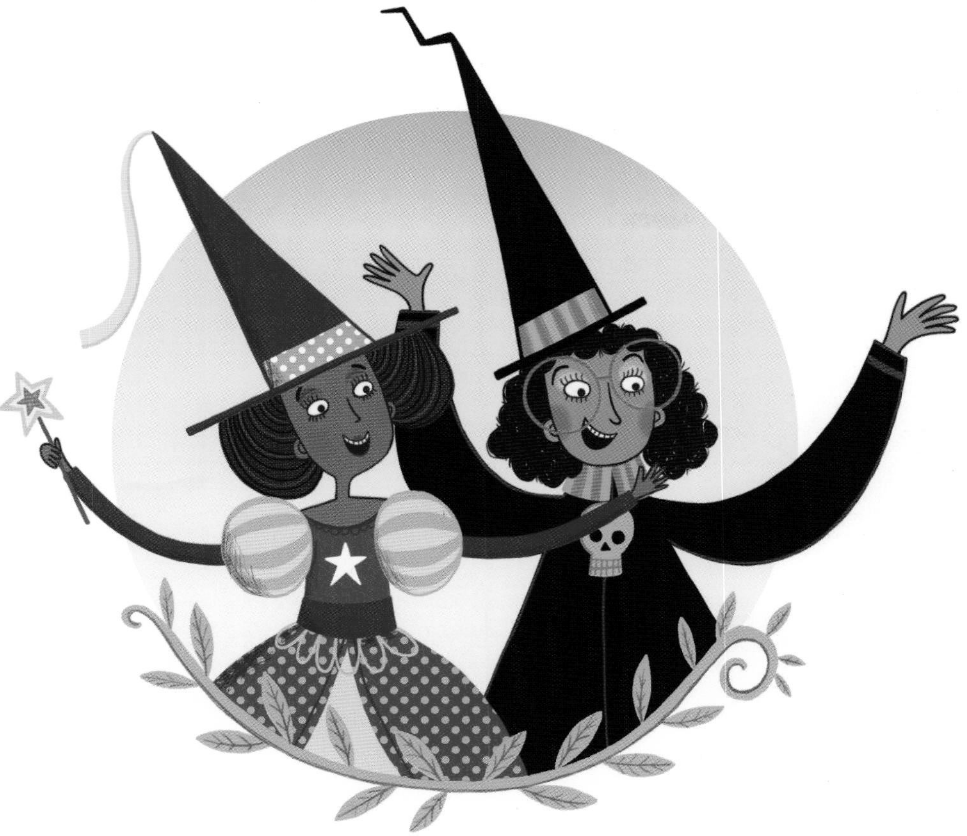

The witches said,
"Welcome!"
then asked,
"Do you fly?"

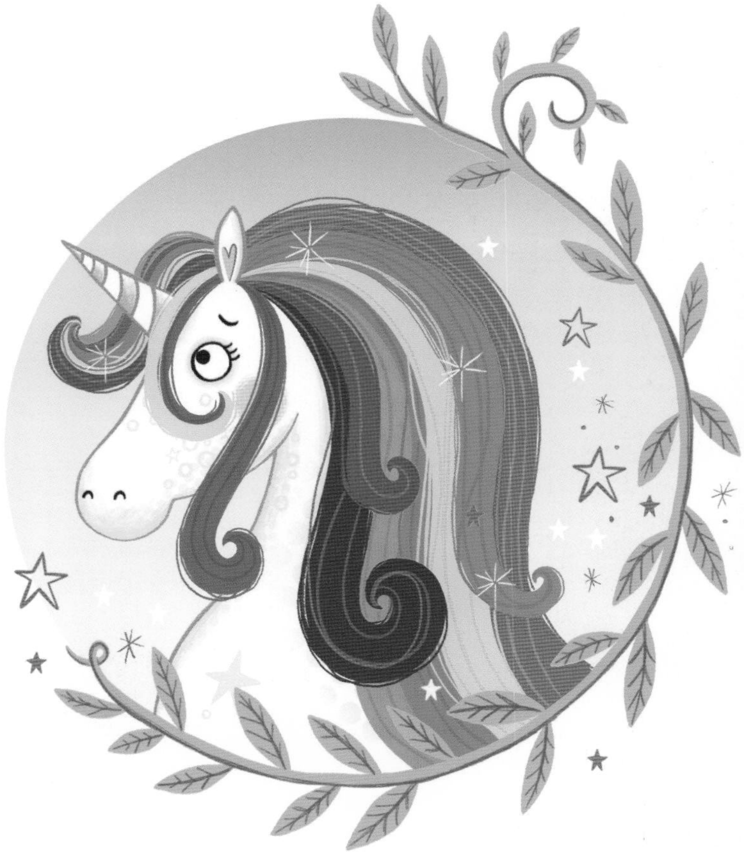

But suddenly Unicorn seemed rather shy.
For just as the elves gave a loud, chorused

"WHOOP!"

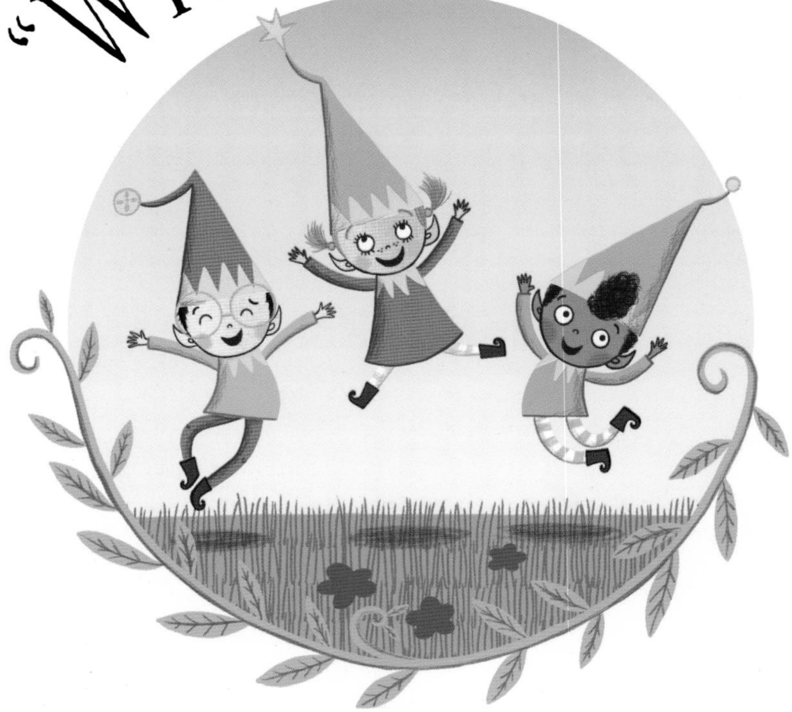

the unicorn let out . . .

. . . A large rainbow poop!

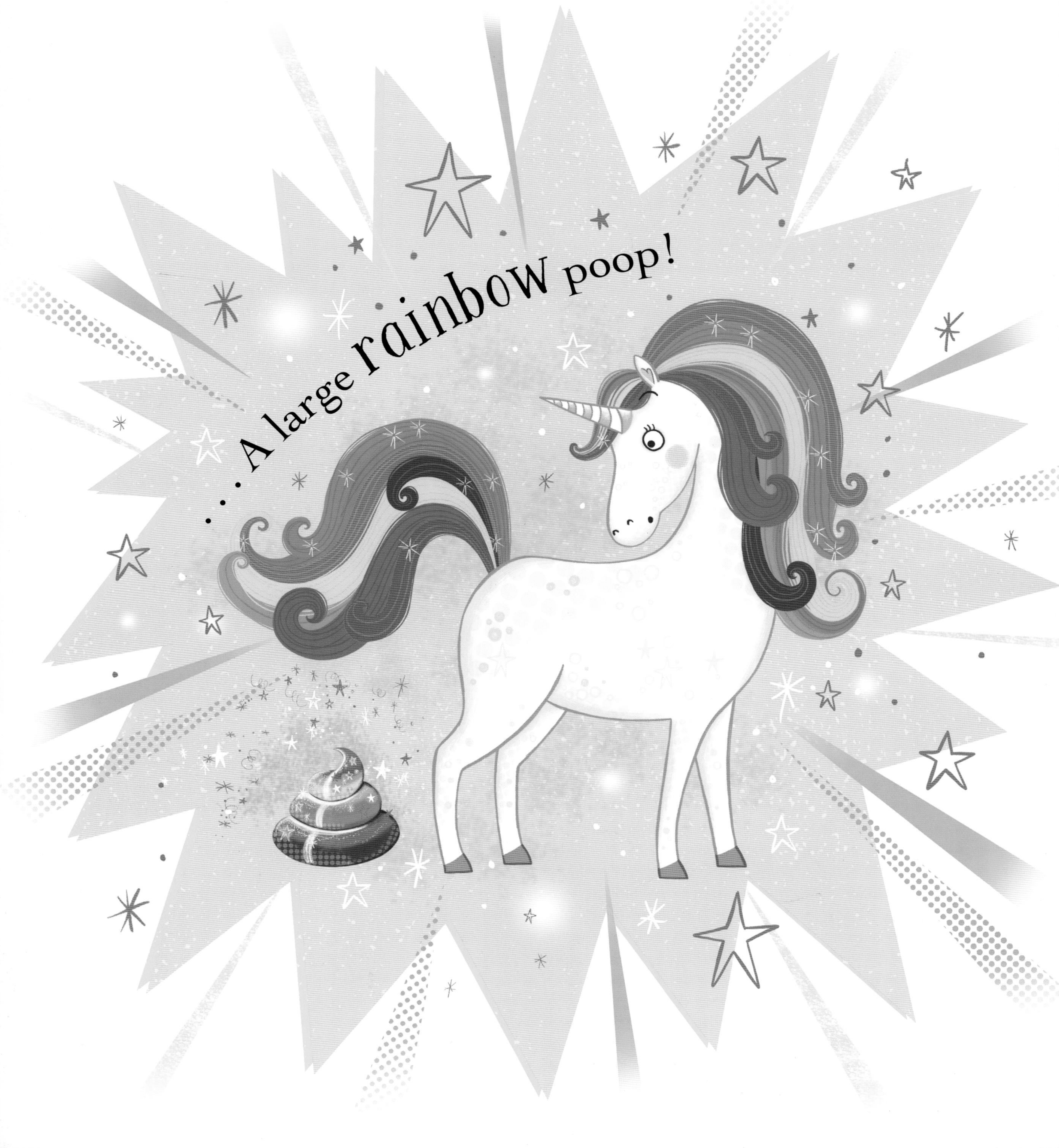

Well! Now, let me tell you, this was a surprise.

The fairies all started to cover their eyes.

The birds disappeared and the dragons flew off.

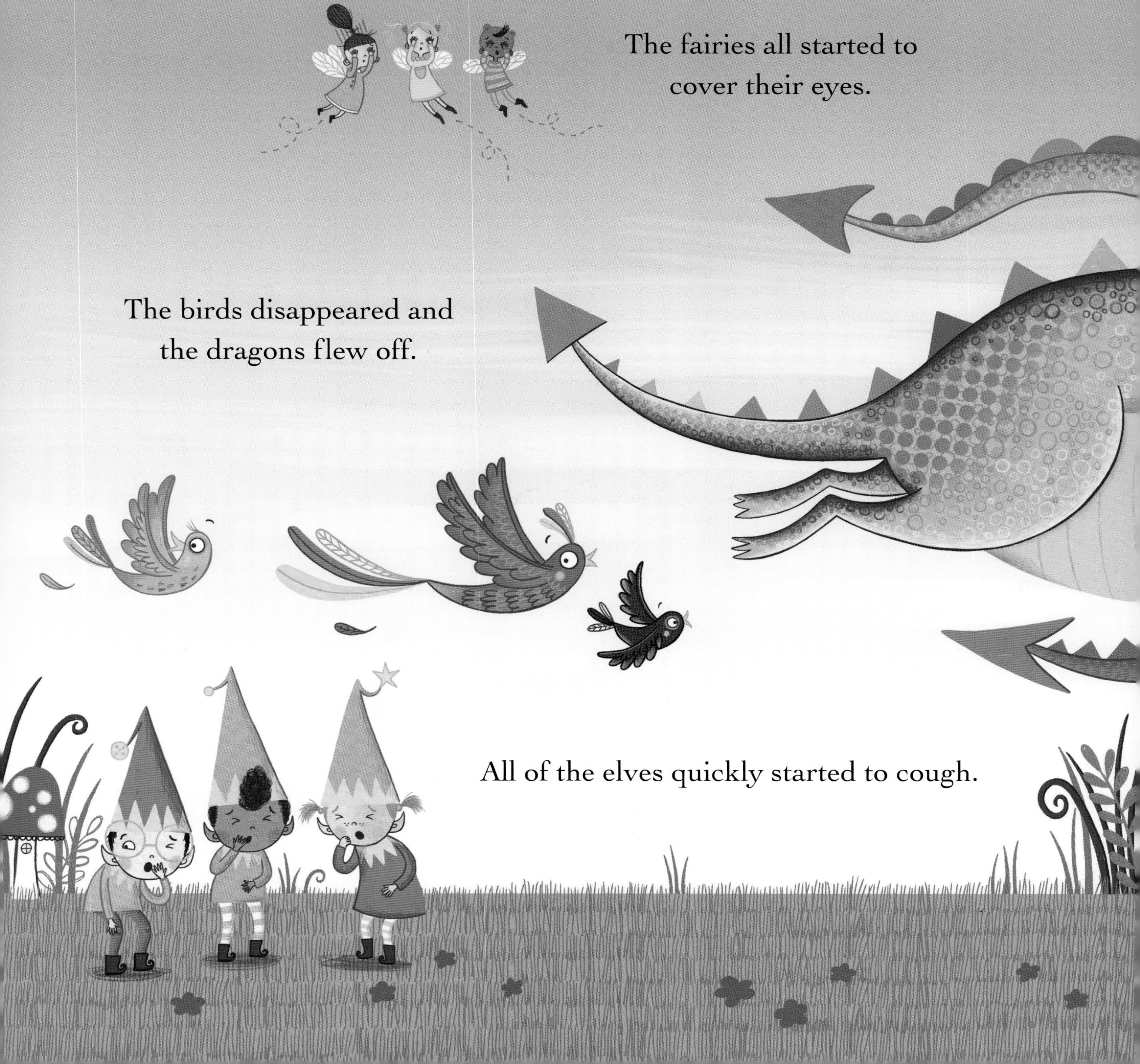

All of the elves quickly started to cough.

"HOLD ON!" called the princess (she needed to yell),

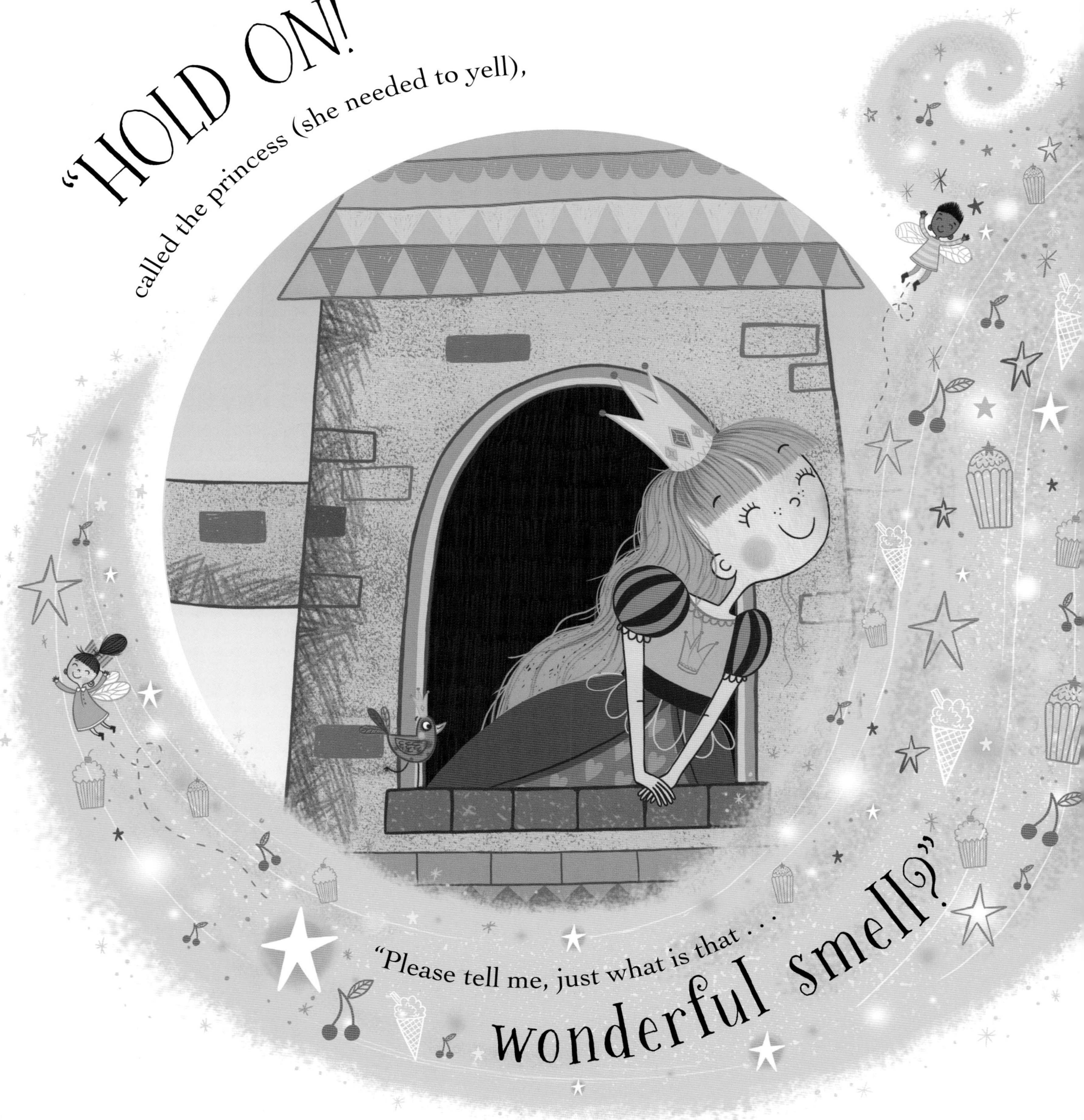

"Please tell me, just what is that . . . wonderful smell?"

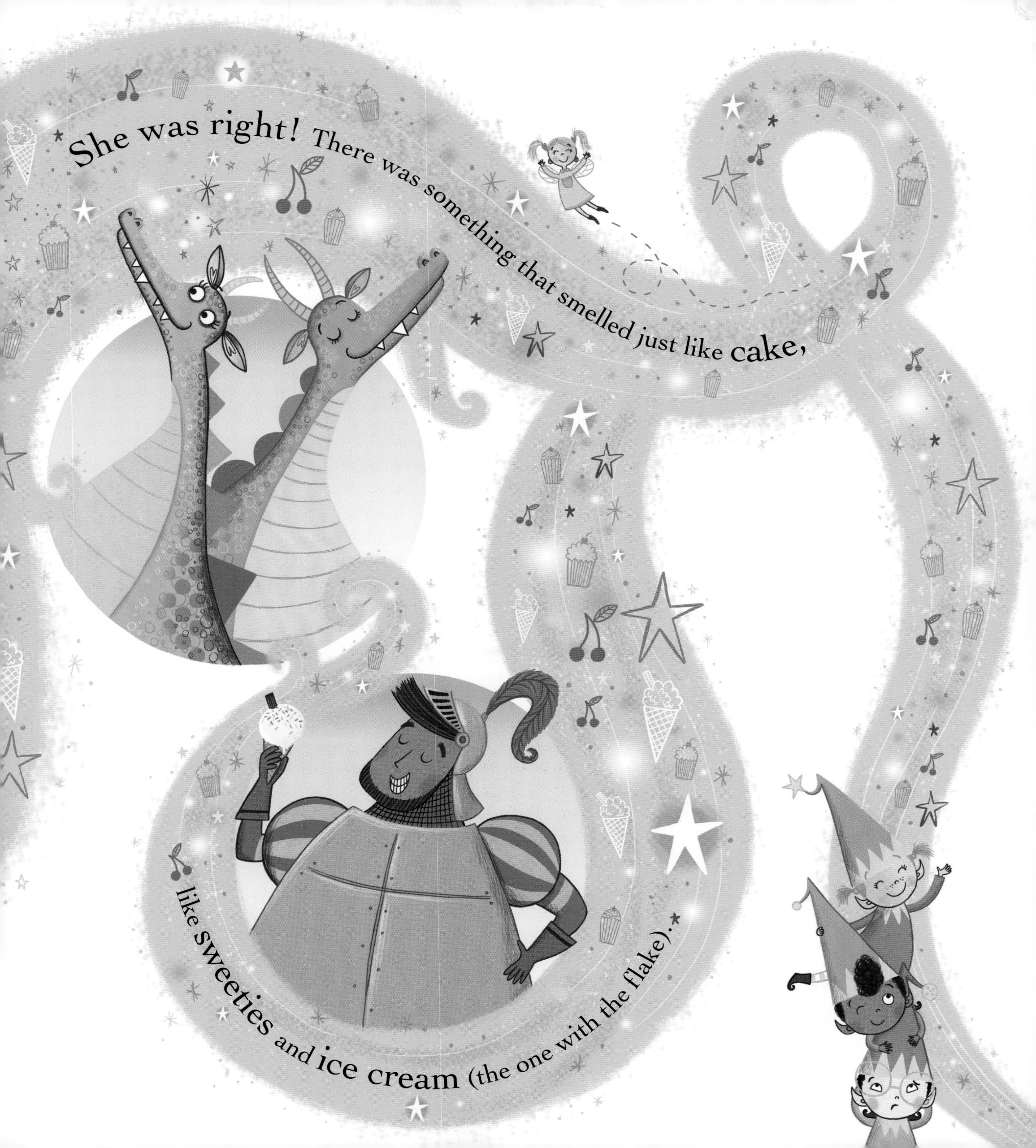

She was right! There was something that smelled just like cake,

like sweeties and ice cream (the one with the flake)...

And then they all realised
– it was very clear.
The **magnificent smell**,
it was coming from …

HERE!

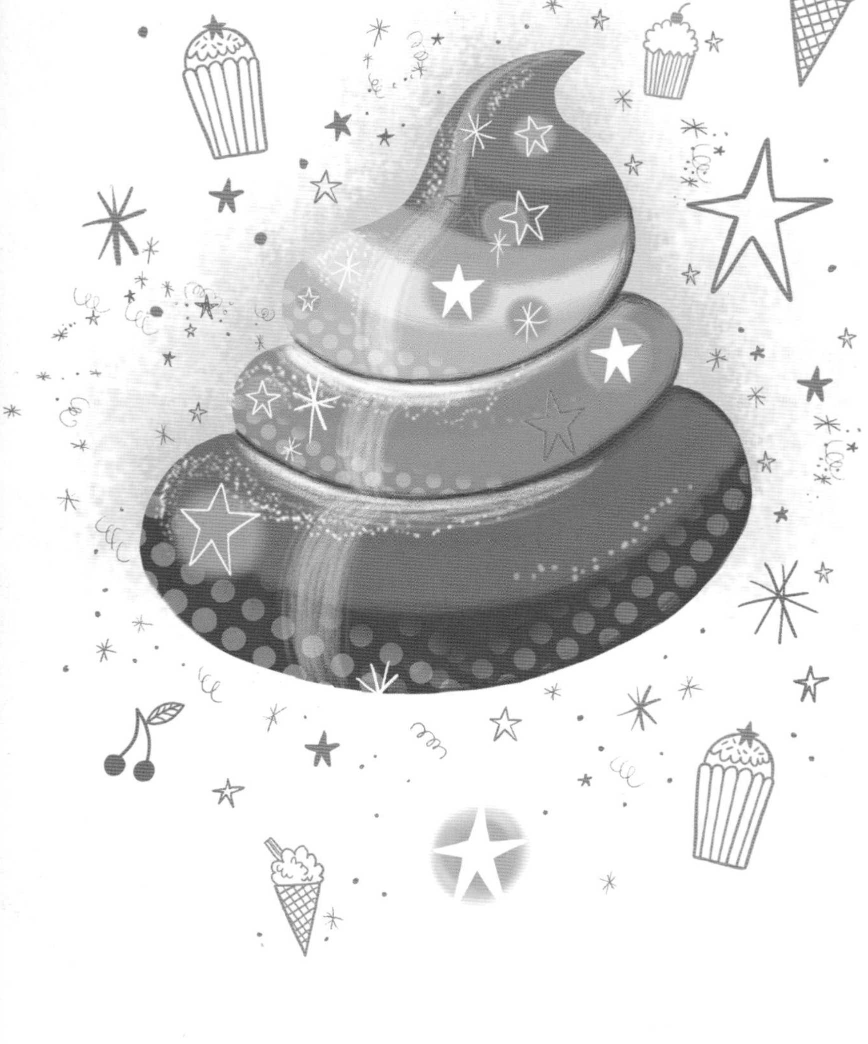

As soon as the rainbow poop
touched to the ground
the most **beautiful colours,**
they spread all around.

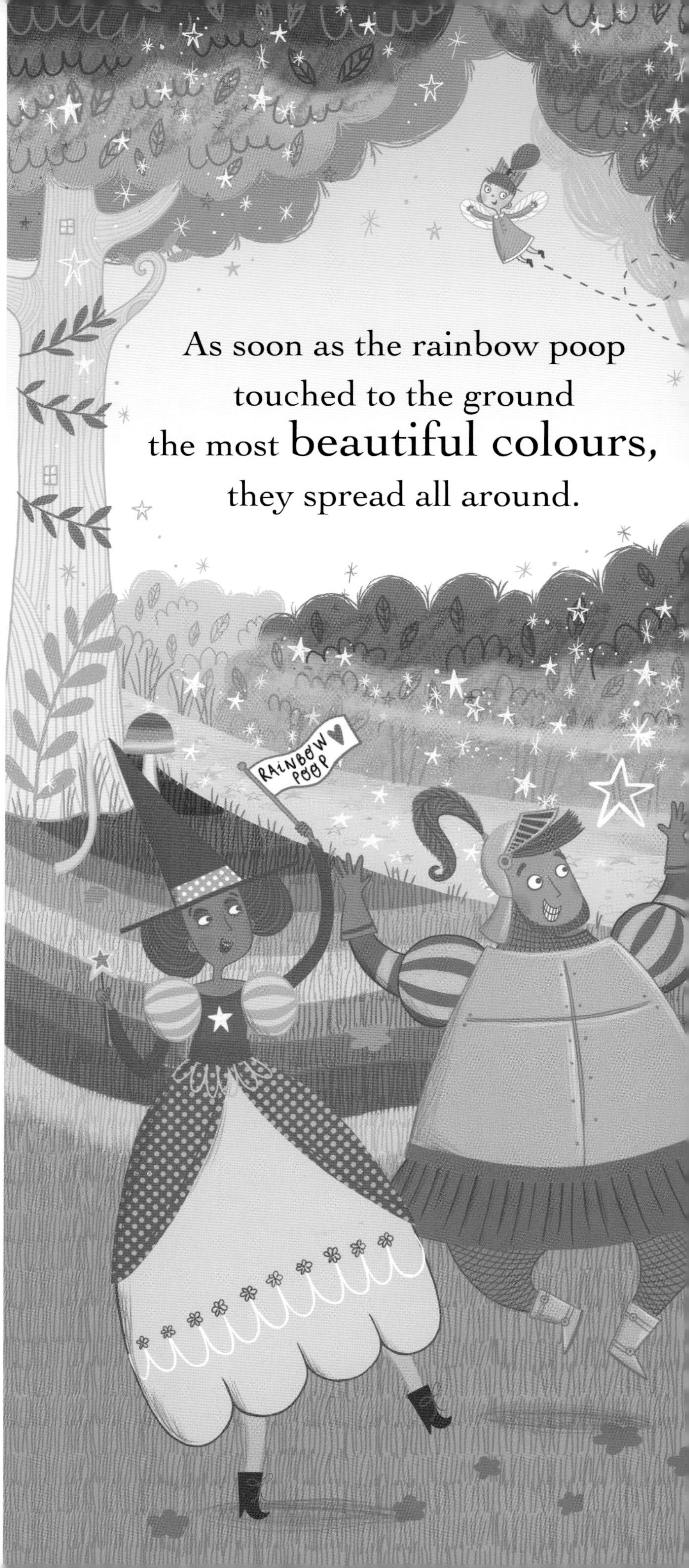
RAINBOW POOP

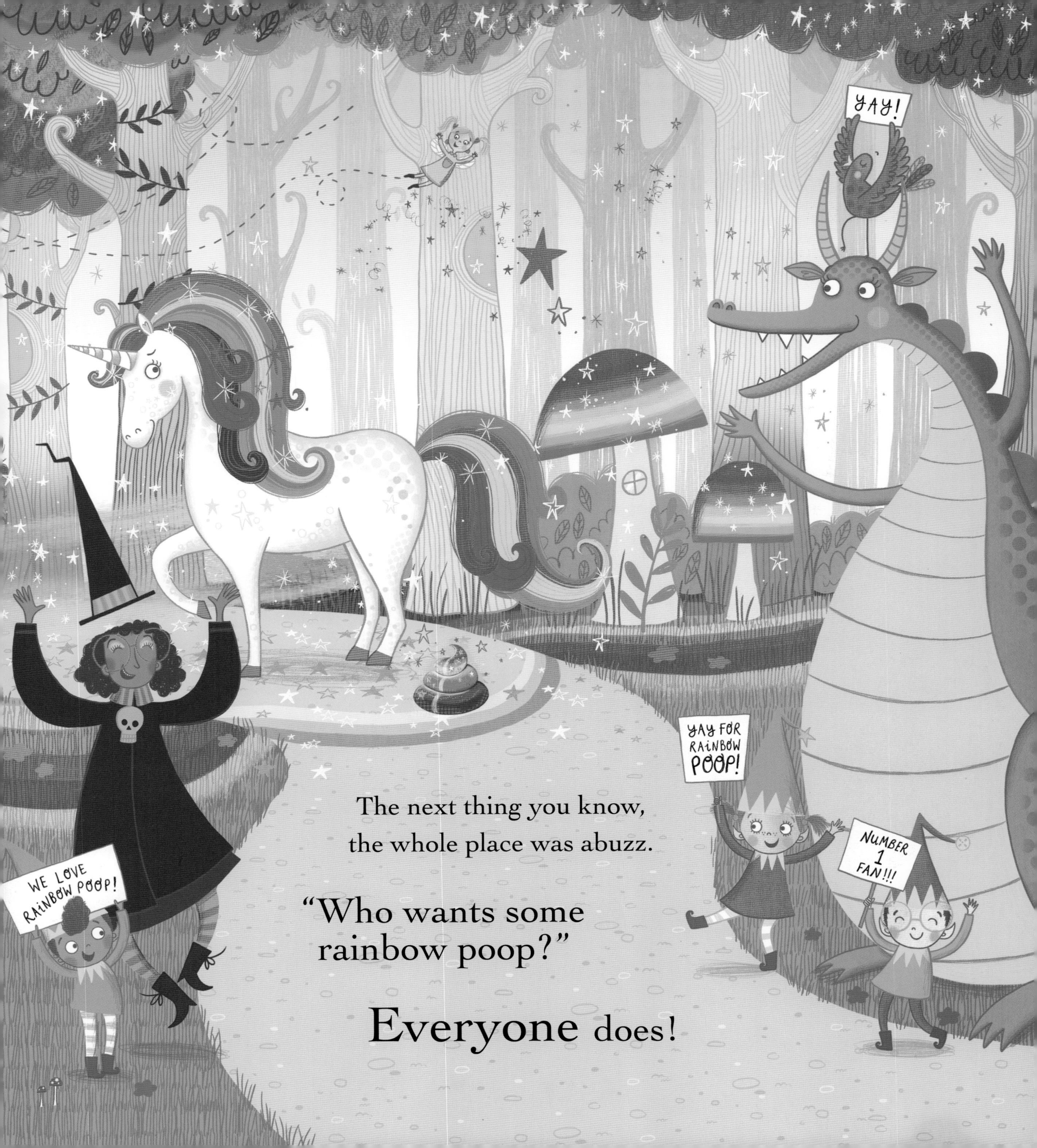
YAY!
YAY FOR RAINBOW POOP!
NUMBER 1 FAN!!!
WE LOVE RAINBOW POOP!

The next thing you know,
the whole place was abuzz.

"Who wants some
rainbow poop?"

Everyone does!

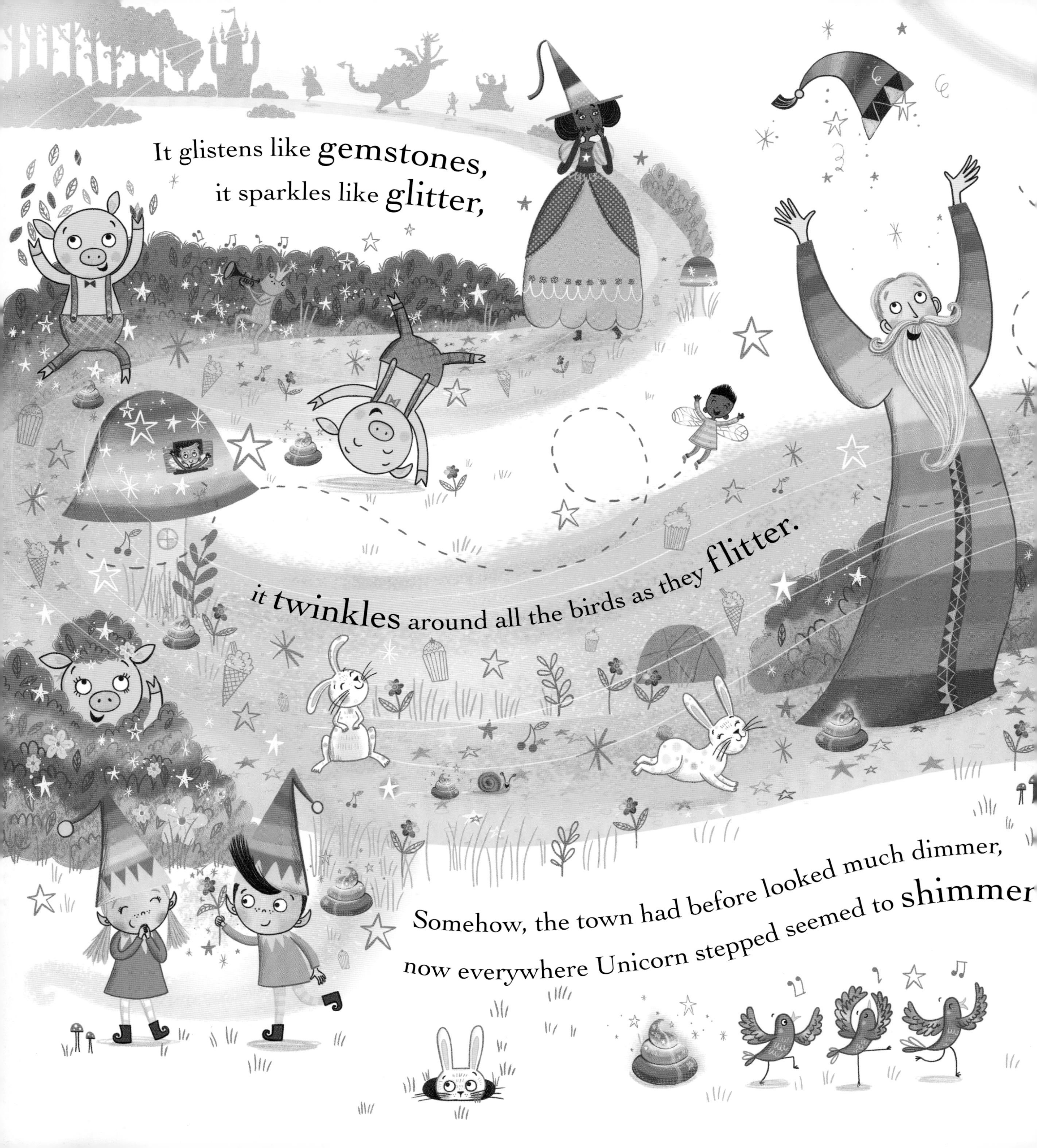

It glistens like gemstones,
it sparkles like glitter,
it twinkles around all the birds as they flitter.

Somehow, the town had before looked much dimmer,
now everywhere Unicorn stepped seemed to shimmer

The scent was delicious, the colours so bright,
"I love rainbow poop!"
shouted out Mr Knight.

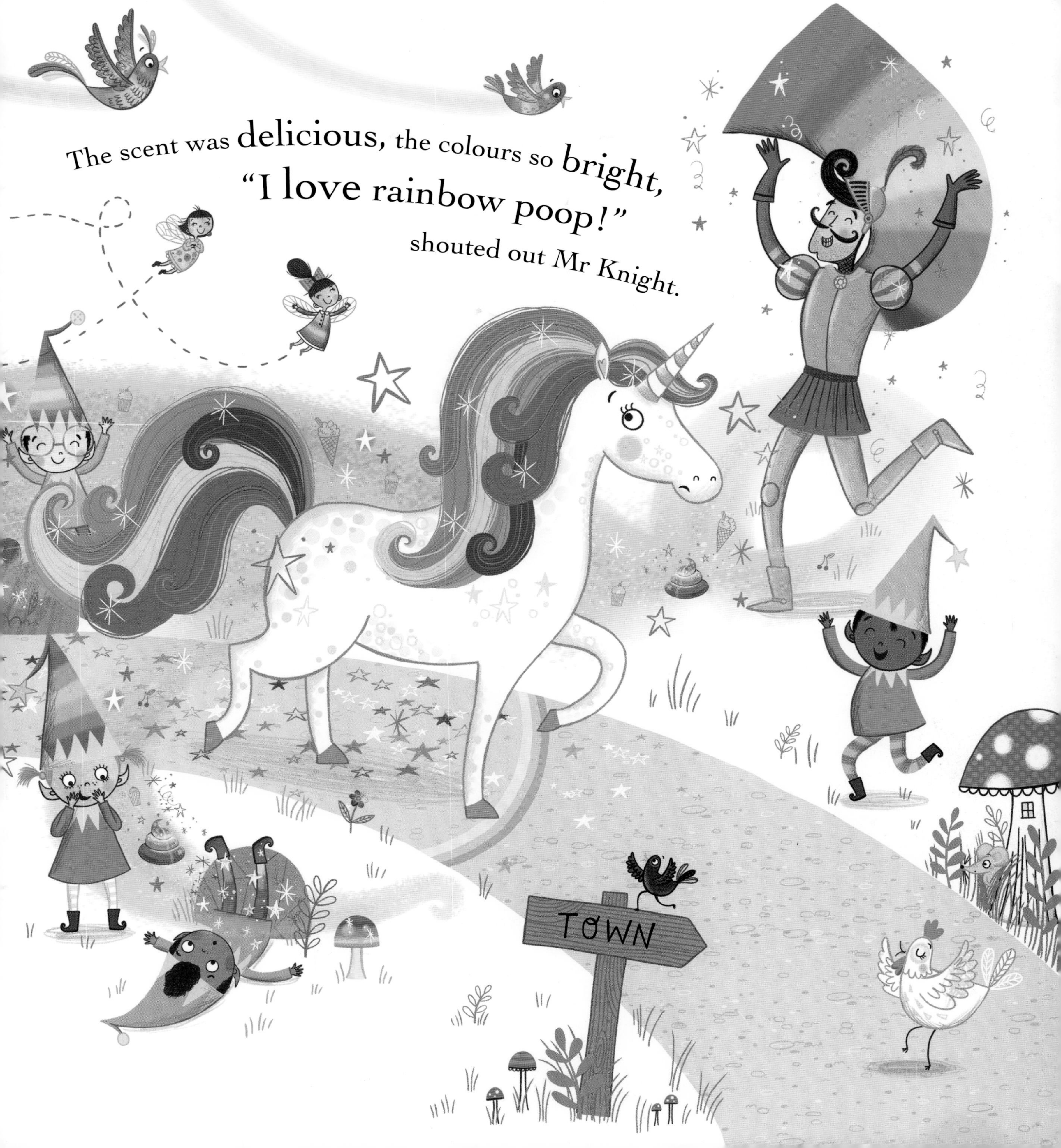
TOWN

The townsfolk felt **giddy**, oh my what a sight!
This sweet-smelling rainbow was such a **delight**!

But . . .

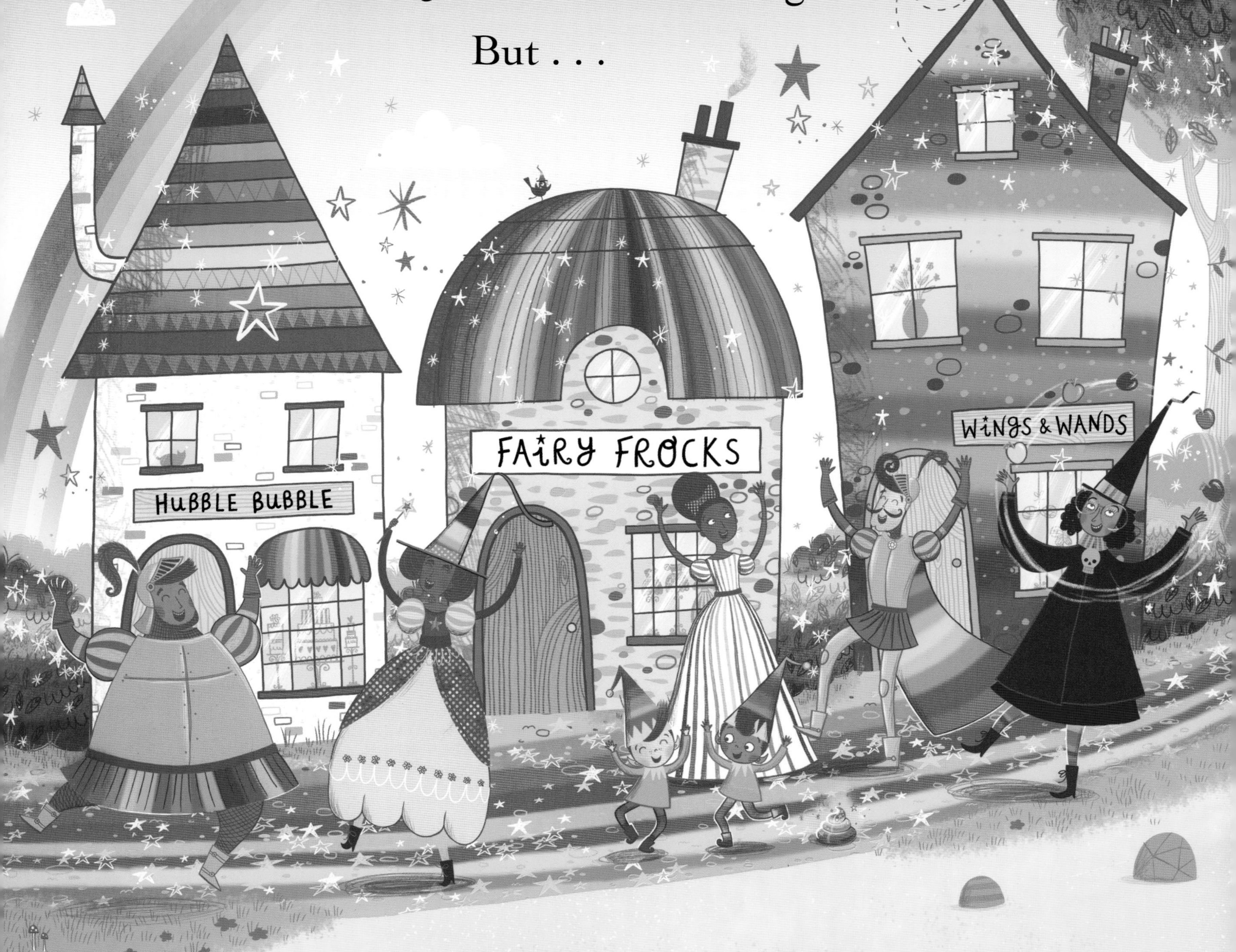
HUBBLE BUBBLE
FAIRY FROCKS
WINGS & WANDS

Unicorn's smile had turned into a **frown**.
Her new friends were making her feel rather down.
She knew that her rainbow poop had caused a stir,
but everyone seemed to like **poop** more than her.

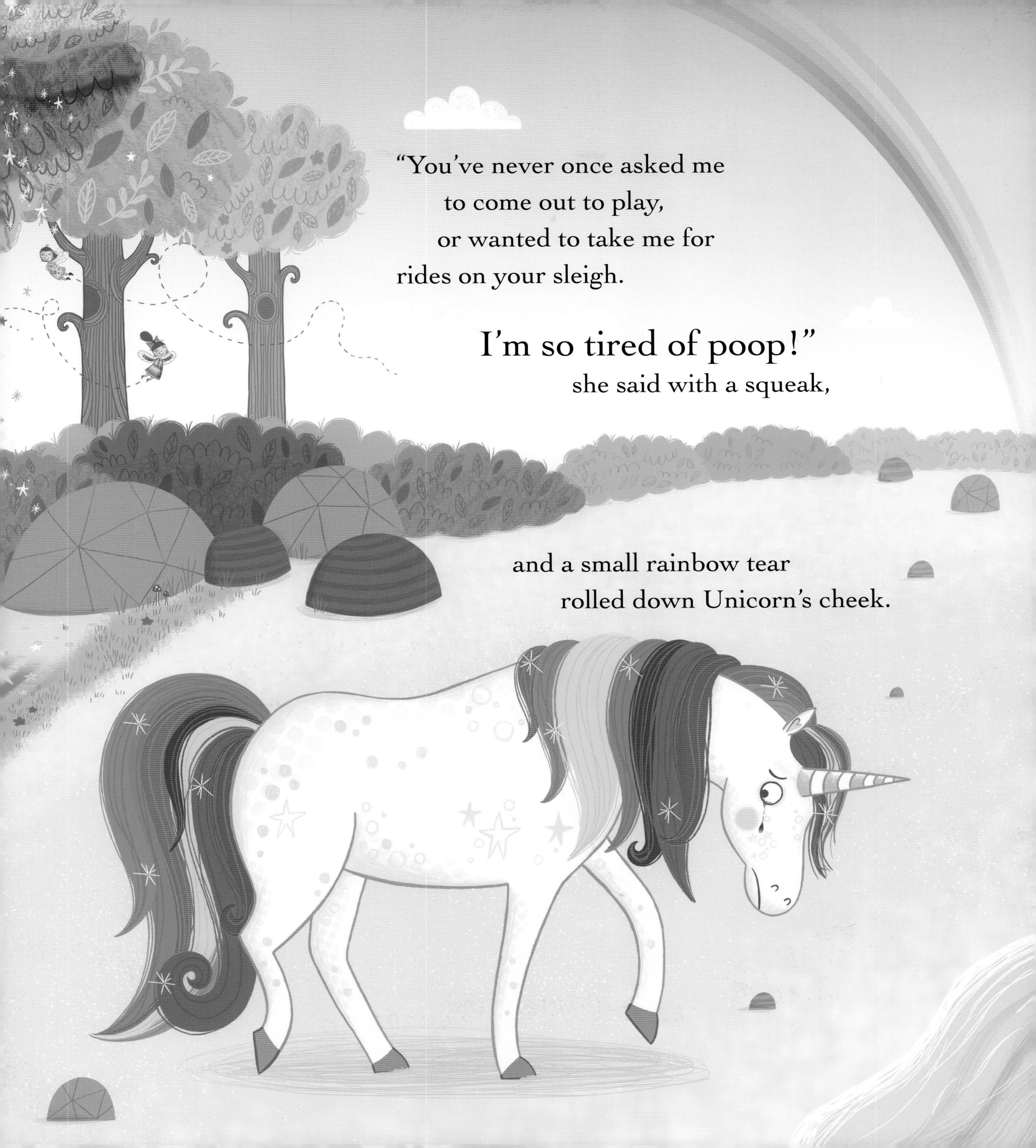

"You've never once asked me
to come out to play,
or wanted to take me for
rides on your sleigh.

I'm so tired of poop!"
she said with a squeak,

and a small rainbow tear
rolled down Unicorn's cheek.

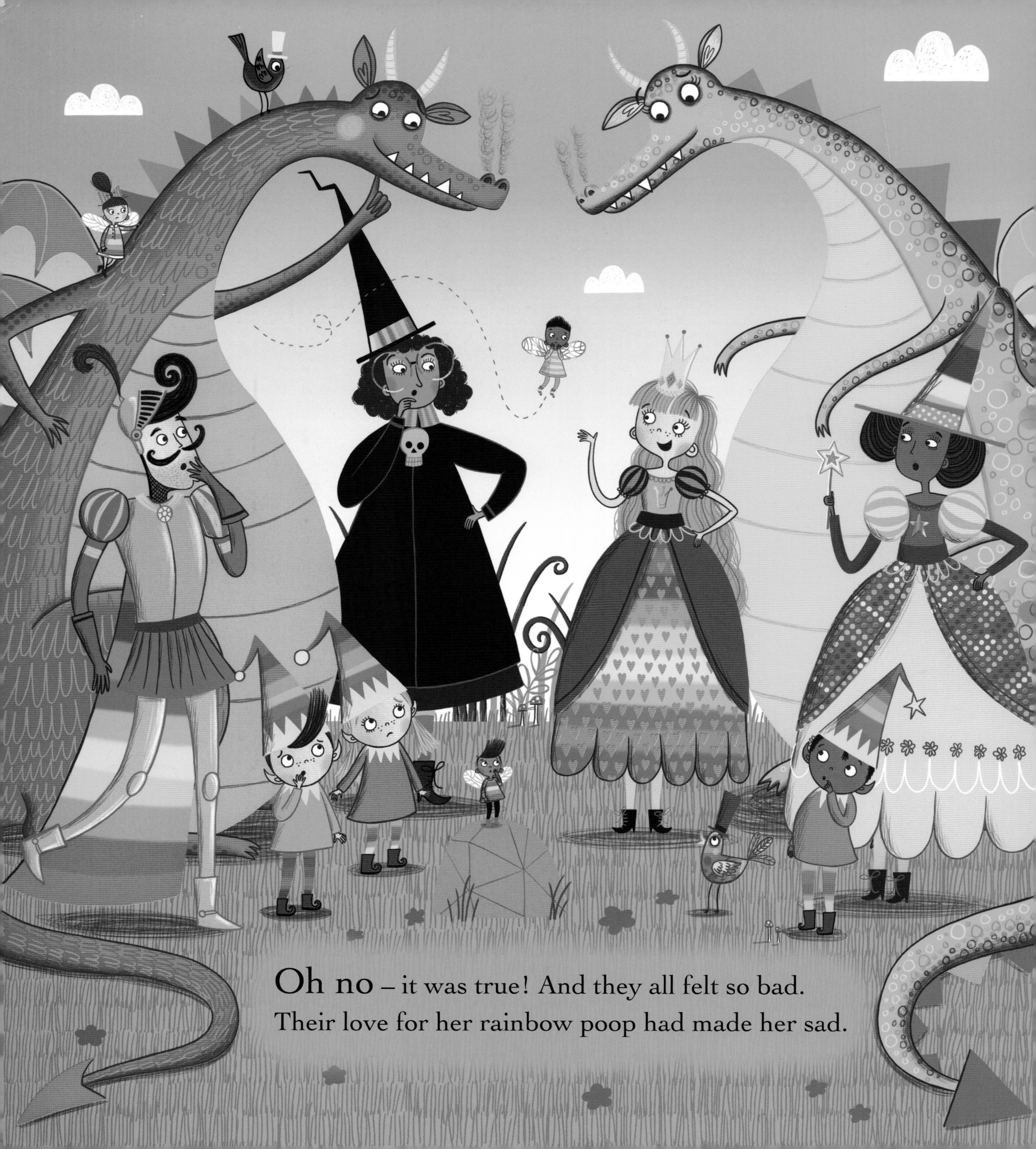

Oh no – it was true! And they all felt so bad.
Their love for her rainbow poop had made her sad.

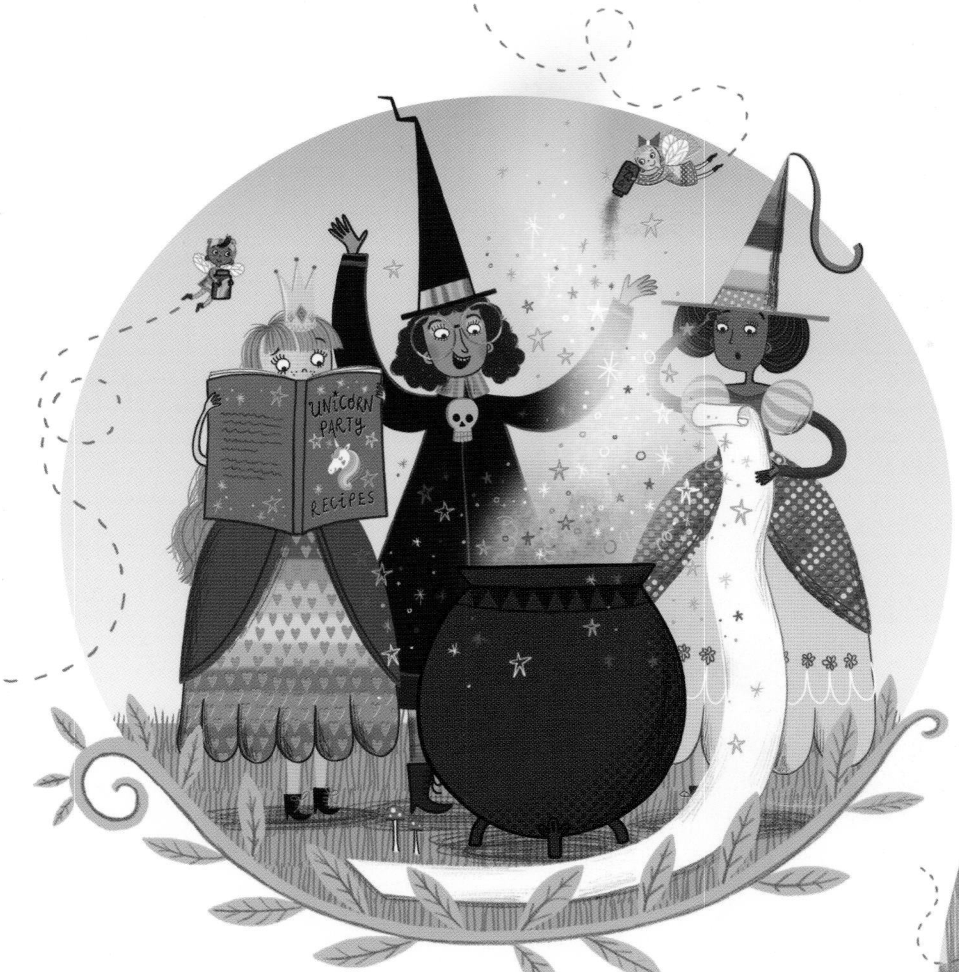
UNICORN
PARTY
RECIPES

They planned a **big** party
and she had no clue.

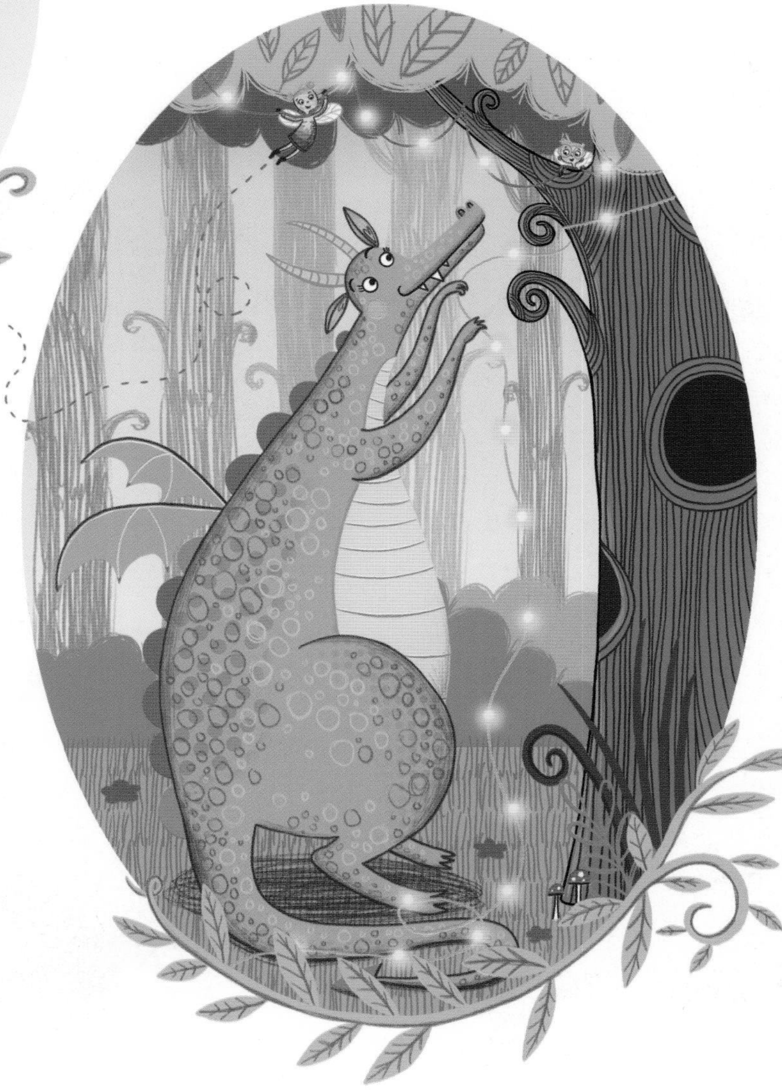

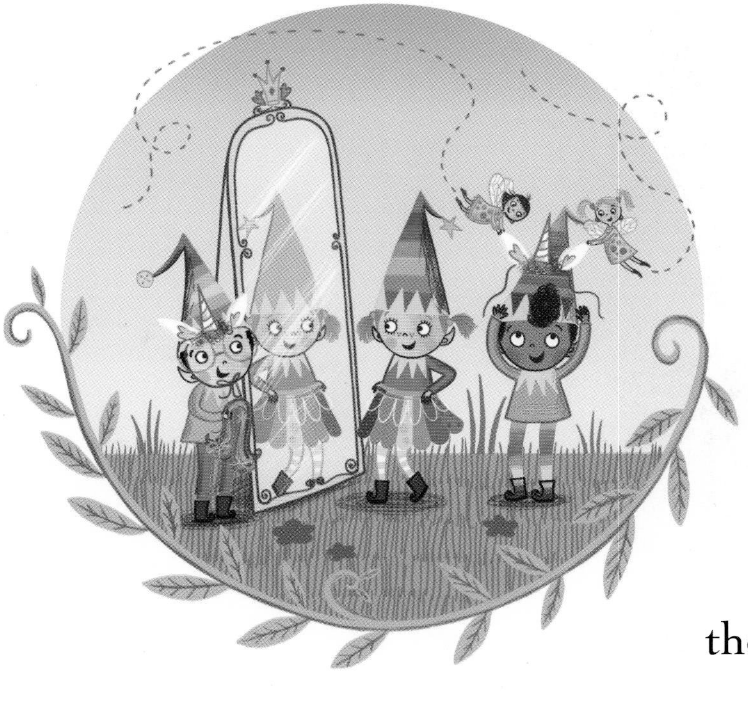

then they all said a very
big, honest . . .

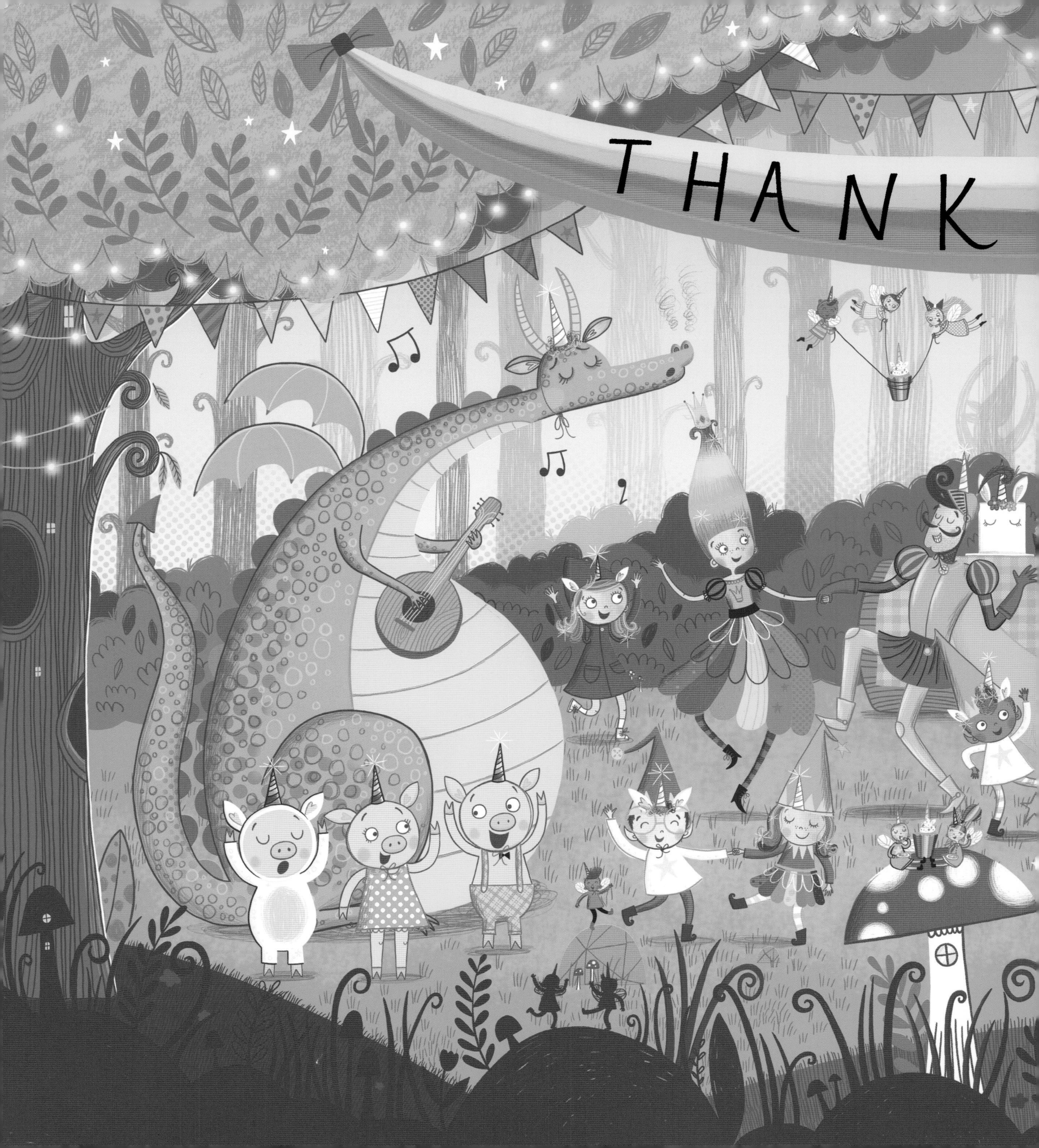
THANK

you!

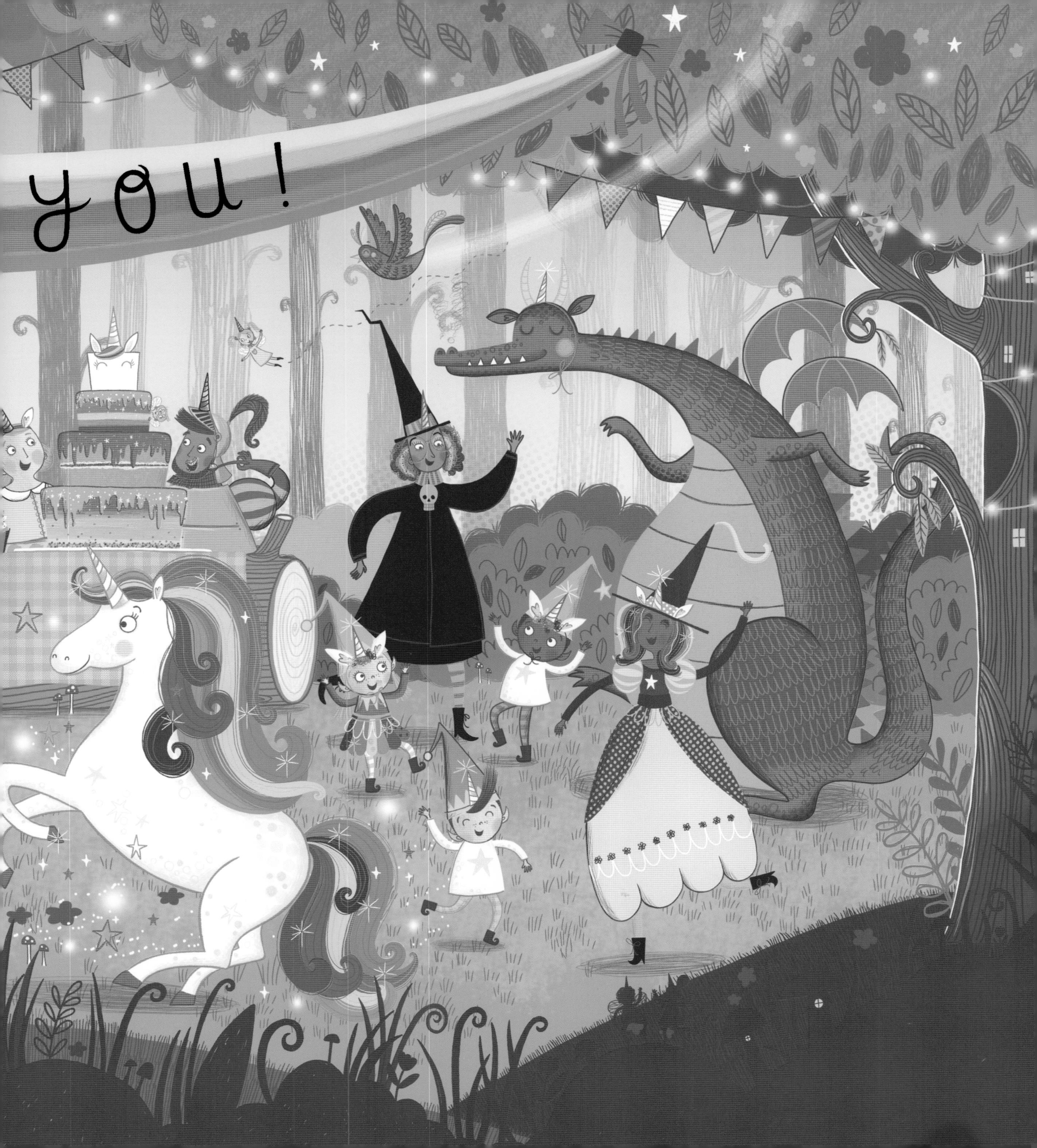

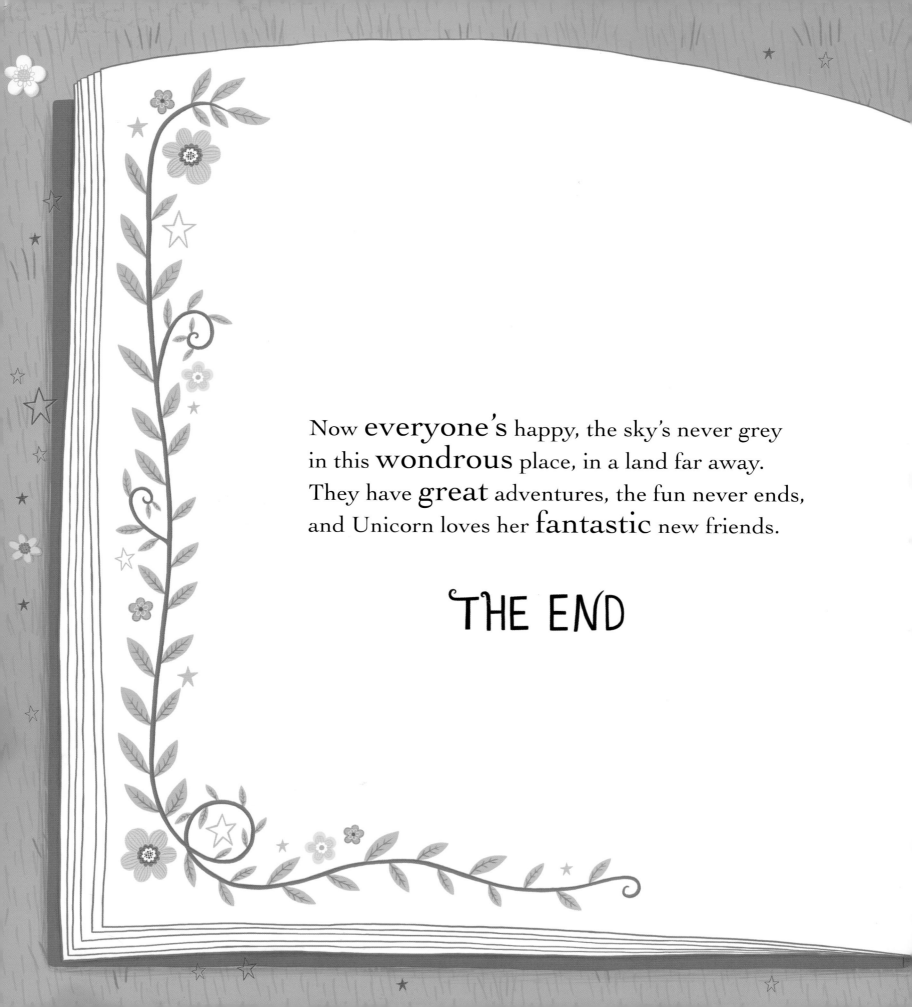

Now everyone's happy, the sky's never grey
in this wondrous place, in a land far away.
They have great adventures, the fun never ends,
and Unicorn loves her fantastic new friends.

THE END

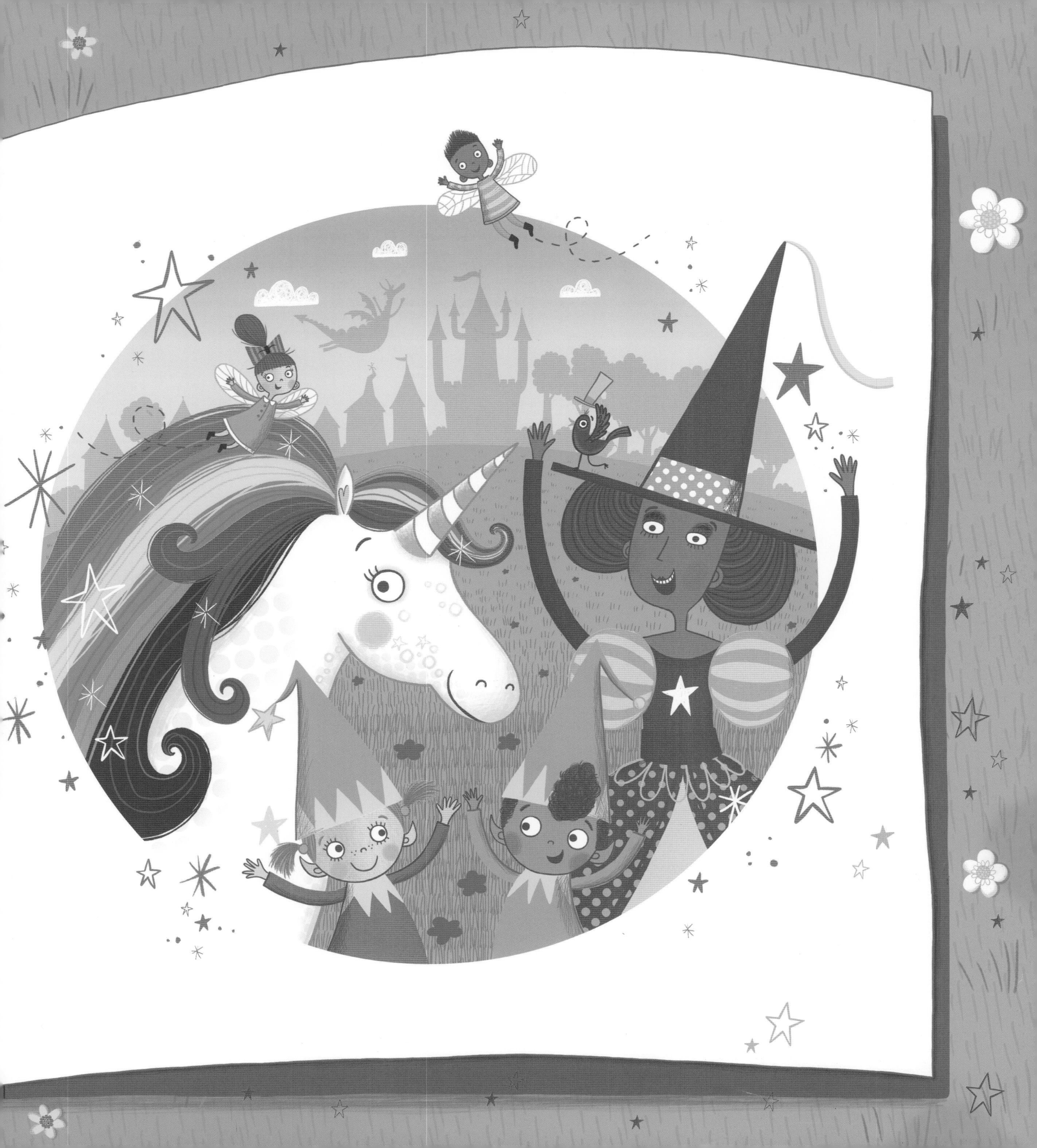

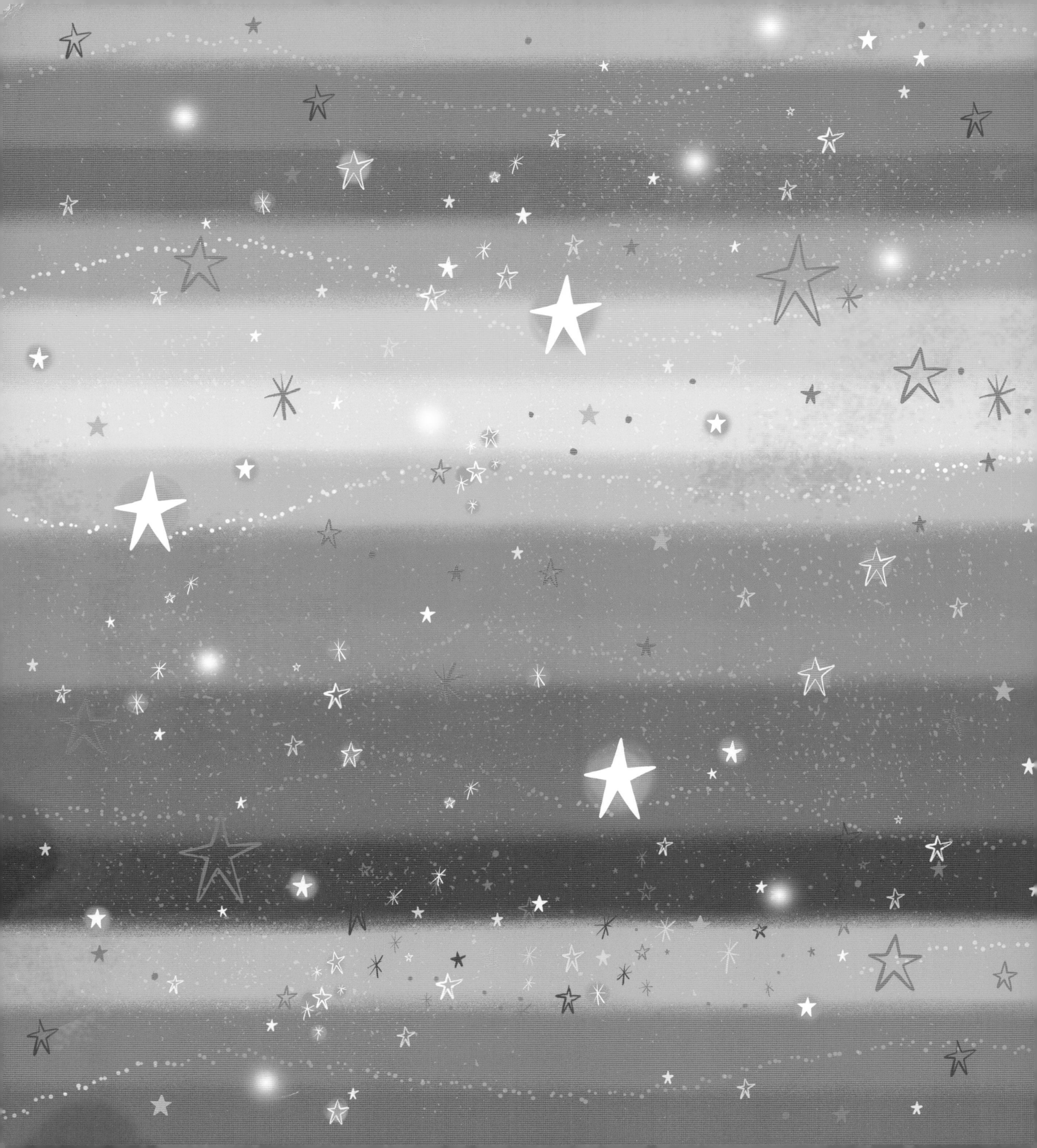

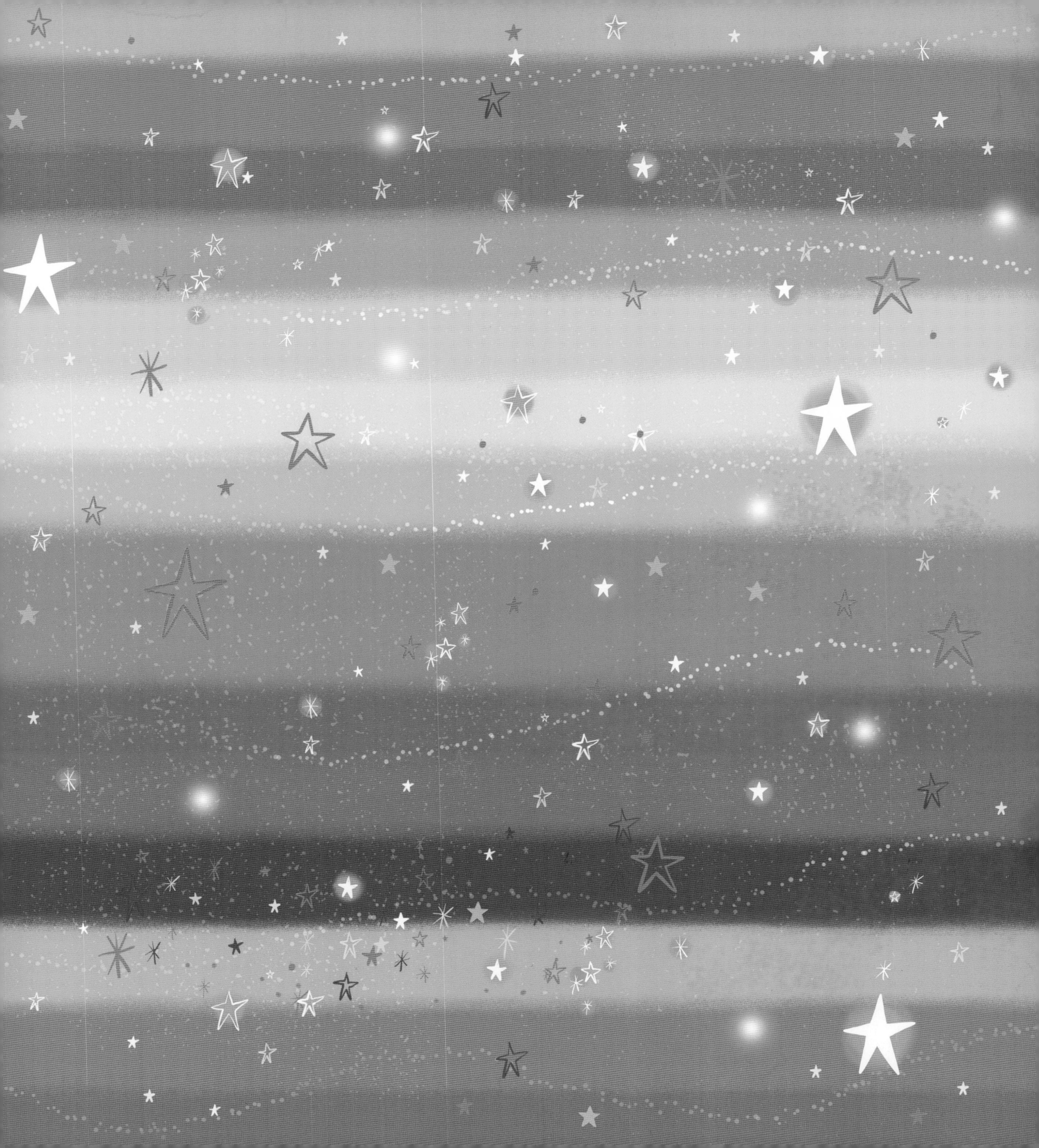